Murder at Mountjoy Manor

Elizabeth Ducie

A Chudleigh Phoenix Publications Book

Cover design: Berni Stevens

Map of Coombesford: Otis Lea-Weston

ISBN: 978-1-913020-10-1

Chudleigh Phoenix Publications

For all the friends who made us feel so welcome when we moved to Devon

The Village of Coombesford

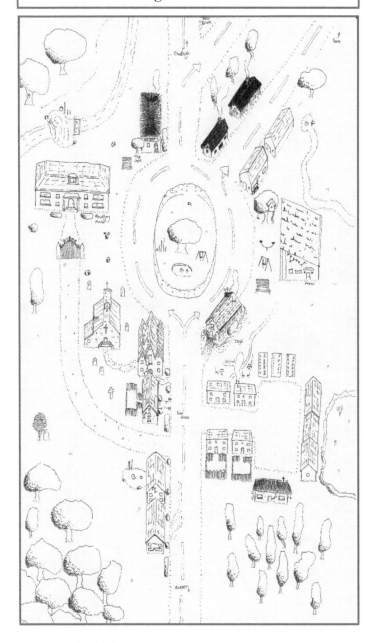

PROLOGUE: MONDAY 8TH JULY 2019

As Charlie Jones crossed the beer garden and headed downhill in search of fresh flowers for the breakfast tables, the faint traffic noise faded. Coombesford was located along the side of a valley; the stream at its base meandering through the fields to join the River Teign on the other side of Chudleigh. The Falls, a gastropub with rooms, got its name from a series of weirs carrying the water from its high point in the hills behind Mountjoy Manor. At this time of year the water was low, and little more than a gentle splashing greeted Charlie's ears.

Reaching up to pluck some spikes of buddleia from a large bush, she glanced towards the stream, as something caught her eye. It looked as if someone had dumped a bag of rubbish in the water. But why would a bag of rubbish have arms? Dropping the flowers, she ran down towards the water's edge. The ground was hard and dry, and as her trainers hit a patch of loose dirt, she felt her feet slip from under her. She slid down the side of the bank and, grabbing at an overhanging branch, skidded to a halt as her toes hit the water.

The body was caught in the reeds and lay face down in a few centimetres of water. The current parted around the head, swirled and eddied along the torso, and rejoined at the feet to continue on its way, as though there was nothing to disturb the flow. Charlie could see it was a man, although his face was hidden. Despite the bloody hole at the back of his skull, she bent and placed two fingertips gently on the pulse point just below his left ear. There was nothing.

Sitting back on the bank, she pulled her phone from her pocket and pressed speed dial.

"Annie, it's me. There's a body in the water at the foot of the falls. I'm going to call the emergency services and stay until they arrive. You'll have to cover for me at breakfast." She listened to the voice at the other end, shaking her head. "Yes, I know the guests will probably notice something's going on, but don't tell them anything for the moment." She was about to disconnect, when she had another thought. "And, Annie; make sure Suzy stays with you in the main building until she's ready for school. I don't want her coming down here right now."

A sudden eddy caught the torso and twisted it round. Horrified, Charlie found herself looking into the bruised and battered face of Simon Mountjoy.

CHAPTER 1: SEVEN DAYS EARLIER (MONDAY 1ST JULY)

Simon Mountjoy CBE ran down the stairs to the indoor pool, following the sound of laughter and splashing. The staircase ended in a light, airy room, spanning the width of the house. A glass wall to the back overlooked a formal lawn, a hillside running down to a small copse of trees and out across the valley onto Dartmoor. The rest of the walls were painted to resemble a Roman villa, with fake pillars and statues of the deities. There was a faint smell of chlorine in the air. The floor area was mainly taken up with a swimming pool, surrounded by white loungers and tables. A woman was swimming rapidly along the length of the pool, a tanned young man encouraging her from the poolside. He had curly black hair which he pushed out of his eyes as he looked up at Simon, and a neatly trimmed beard and moustache.

"Olga," Simon called, "can you get out of the water, please? I need to talk to you."

The second Mrs Mountjoy swam lazily to the steps and pulled herself out of the water. She was topless and wore just the briefest of bikini bottoms. Her breasts were magnificent, lightly tanned without the hint of a strap-mark, and she wore a sparkling ruby in her navel. As she pushed her hair back from her face, matching stones in rows of

3

studs flashed at her ears. Simon coughed and glanced quickly at the young man who was grinning at him. Seeing her husband's embarrassment, the woman laughed and her companion joined in. He picked up a robe and held it out for her.

"Thank you, Nathan darling," Olga Mountjoy purred as she slipped her arms into the sleeves. She let her fingers linger for a few seconds on his outstretched arm; then, tying the belt around her waist, she walked across and blew a kiss in Simon's direction, before sinking onto one of the loungers, inviting him to join her.

"What do you want to talk about, then?" she asked. Simon glanced at the young man and raised his eyebrows. Olga sighed. "You'd better disappear, darling," she said, fluttering her hand in his direction. "My husband wants to talk to me in private. Go and lift some weights or something." The young man sniffed in obvious disapproval at his dismissal, raked his fingers through his curls once more and headed back upstairs into the house. "Now, what do you want to talk about?" she repeated.

"I really don't think you should be wandering around topless in front of the staff, Olga, do you?"

Olga sniggered.

"Nathan's not staff, darling. He's my personal trainer; he's practically one of the family." She sniggered again. "Let's face it, his hands touch me more than yours these days. I've no secrets from him." She shook her head. "You English are so stuffy. Back home in Ukraine, we've got mixed saunas. We're not ashamed of our bodies!"

"Well, you're not back home in Ukraine now, and I expect you to behave with some decorum! Is that clear? Especially while the film crew's here."

"You've got a date then?" Olga sat up, her teasing look gone. "When are they coming? How long will they be here? And will they be interviewing us together or separately?"

Simon was relieved to see his wife was taking this documentary project seriously. Thirteen years he'd been

4

working on reclaiming his family home and this was the way he would show the world he'd succeeded.

"They'll be here first thing on Wednesday, and expect to finish the first phase at the weekend. I thought we could throw a lunch party for them on Sunday, before they head back to London."

"Sounds good. And our interviews?"

"I haven't finalised the timetable with them yet, Olga. But it'll probably be some time on Friday. They're going to start with the outside shots and then move inside later on. We can do the interviews wherever you feel most comfortable." He shook a finger at her as he stood up. "Just so long as you're fully clothed!"

"Yes, Mr Mountjoy, sir," she said, throwing him a mock salute. She uncurled herself from the lounger, stretched, dropped her robe to her feet, and strolled across to kiss him lingeringly before diving back into the pool and swimming half a length under water. Surfacing and pushing her hair back off her face, she called out, "can you send Nathan back down if you see him? I need some more exercise." And flashing him a seductive smile that, together with the kiss, reminded him just why he'd been attracted to this woman in the first place, she turned away and continued swimming.

CHAPTER 2

When Simon reached the top of the stairs and re-entered the main house, he found the bi-fold doors to the terrace thrown open. Nathan was outside, lifting a set of weights with the ease of someone who spent a lot of time building up his strength. Simon stood in the shadows and watched him for a while. The young man was standing sideways to the door and appeared to be admiring his reflection in the glass.

Nathan Williams had arrived out of the blue one day in March, when Olga was advertising for a personal trainer. Initially he'd just visited a couple of times a week, from his rented accommodation in Exeter, but gradually he spent more and more time at Mountjoy Manor and Olga suggested it would be easier if he had one of the spare rooms on the second floor.

"After all, darling," she'd said when Simon questioned whether that was really necessary, "Hilda has a room up there; why not Nathan?" Simon didn't bother to point out the difference between a trusted executive assistant who'd worked with and for him since the 1970s, and a young man they knew nothing about. He'd learned the way to keep Olga happy was to let her have her own way on the small things and make her think the bigger things had been her idea in the first place.

Now he coughed to announce his presence, and was amused to see the younger man jump slightly and drop the weights to the ground.

"Olga wants you back down in the pool room, Nathan. She's ready to carry on with her exercises."

"I bet she is," the young man said, raising an eyebrow. Then he jumped again as Simon brought his hand down sharply on the table.

"For some reason, young man, my wife seems to rate you highly, and if it keeps her happy, you can stay," he spat through gritted teeth. "But bear in mind I don't see things in quite the same way. So, I want you to be very careful. Do you understand?" He pointed a finger at Nathan's gleaming, tanned chest. "Don't get too attached to this job; and certainly don't get too attached to my wife. Because I'll be watching you – and if I find any cause, you'll be gone. Trust me on that!" Simon turned on his heel and walked back into the house. As he did, he caught sight of Nathan's reflection in the glass door. He was smirking again. Simon growled to himself. It looked as if this might be a situation he needed to sort out. But it could wait until after the weekend. He didn't want anything to disrupt the harmony of Mountjoy Manor while the film crew was here.

As Simon waited for the coffee machine to do its stuff, he heard Nathan cross the kitchen behind him and run down to the pool room. Olga must have got out of the water again because he could hear her voice quite clearly floating up the staircase.

"Oh, there's a sulky face! Who's upset my Nathan then?"

"Who do you think?" came the reply. "The old man just had a go at me. He thinks there's something going on between us! Threatened to sack me!"

Olga laughed.

"Oh, darling, you don't need to worry about Simon. What's that English saying about dogs barking but not biting?"

"His bark is worse than his bite?"

"That's it. My Simon's bark is definitely worse than his bite. And he will do anything for me." There was a pause and Simon wondered just what was going on down there. But then he heard a familiar clicking and realised Olga was just lighting a cigarette. "Besides," she went on, "you work for me. So no-one can take your job away from you—apart from me. Okay?"

"Fair enough," said Nathan. "Right, enough relaxation; time to get that gorgeous body of yours exercising again. Back in the water, please." There was a muted splash, followed by the sound of Olga powering up and down the length of the pool once more.

As Simon stirred cream into his coffee and strolled towards the hallway, he felt a tremor of pure anger course through his body.

CHAPTER 3

Hilda Reynolds looked up as the door flew open and Simon strode in. Oh dear, this didn't look good. She watched as her boss threw himself down in his chair and stirred his coffee with such ferocity, she began to fear for the safety of the mug and its surroundings. She moved a pile of papers away from the danger zone and then, straightening her cardigan and running a hand over her neatly-pinned bun to make sure no hair was out of place, she carried on working on the filming schedule that had arrived by email that morning. She'd learned over the years when to keep absolutely silent.

Glancing out of the window at the mature shrubbery and manicured driveway, she told herself once again how lucky she was to work in such beautiful surroundings. When they'd moved down from London nearly twenty years ago, they'd worked out of a Portacabin on site. But over the years, the large sitting room at the front of the house had been converted into an office and contained everything you would need to run a successful business empire. The renovation had been tasteful and the marble fireplace, detailed coving on the ceiling and period wallpaper meant it maintained an element of elegance that appealed to her. But sometimes, she wished they were back in that anonymous office block in London. Living and working 'over the shop' had definite disadvantages. And she suspected it was one, or maybe two, of those disadvantages that had upset Simon.

Finally, her boss threw his spoon down on the desk and let out a groan.

"Wives! Who'd have them?" Then looking up at her, he smiled ruefully. "Sorry, Hilda, rhetorical question."

Hilda smiled back but said nothing. She knew if Simon wanted to have this conversation, he would say more. And if he didn't, she would just ignore his outburst, as she had so many times over the years.

"You know, Hilda, I realise people think it's amusing, a man in his late sixties with an Eastern European wife half his age. I know they think she's only with me for my money or for the right to live in the UK. But you know what? I don't care. She's great to look at; terrific in…" he shot her a quick glance and maybe realising belatedly where he was, didn't finish the sentence. Hilda could feel herself flushing as he went on. "I've no kids of my own and I've not heard from Lily for years, so she obviously doesn't want anything to do with me. After I'm gone, my money has to go somewhere! So why not to someone who acts the part when I need her to and doesn't bother me too much the rest of the time? We suit each other; we have a mutually beneficial arrangement; and that's all that matters."

"So what's the problem, then? Why so angry?" Hilda's quiet words obviously hit home, as Simon shrugged his shoulders.

"Oh, I don't know. It's that young Nathan Williams. Always fawning over Olga, always smirking at me. I know she loves to tease me and I don't think for one minute there's anything going on between them. She's much too savvy to risk upsetting our arrangement. But I don't like him! And I don't like that he's living here. Olga wants him here, so for the time being, he can stay. But keep your eye on him, won't you? If I get a reason, he'll be out on his ear!"

Simon looked down at his coffee cup and then back up

at Hilda.

"You didn't want coffee, did you?"

"No, it's fine, thank you. I've just finished one." She hadn't, and the aroma from Simon's cup had been calling to her, but she was old-fashioned enough to still feel uncomfortable when the boss offered to make a drink for her. Not that it happened very often. "I've finished annotating the timetable for the filming, if you're ready to go through it?"

"And I've just cleared it with Olga that we'll host the crew for lunch here on Sunday. I know you usually spend the weekends at home, but I'd really appreciate it if you could be there for that. Just in case there are any last minute issues."

"Of course, Simon." Hilda made a mental note to cancel the ticket she'd bought for the lunchtime concert at the Royal Albert Memorial Museum and steeled herself for another missed opportunity to spend time in her little retreat overlooking the Quay in Exeter.

For the rest of the morning, they worked on the plans for the TV documentary which was to be the culmination of Simon's restoration project at Mountjoy Manor. But in the back of her mind, Hilda was replaying Simon's words. He was looking for a reason to get rid of Nathan Williams, was he? That would really upset the Ukrainian princess. Maybe she'd disappear in a huff. If only he'd realised...but Hilda knew she was fooling herself. That ship had sailed many years ago.

And how strange he should talk about Lily today. Hilda didn't think he'd mentioned that name for years.

CHAPTER 4: TUESDAY 2ND JULY

Roger Richardson glanced up from behind his counter as the doorbell pinged. When he saw who was entering, he groaned inwardly, but then breathed a sigh of relief as the newcomer turned right. Wonderful. Let Celia deal with Simon bloody Mountjoy. The less he had to talk to him, the better.

Cosy Corner sat on the edge of the Village Green, next door to the school. It had originally been two buildings, now knocked into one, with the ground-floor rooms connected by a large archway, and a single doorway off the street. To the left, the grocery store was Roger's domain. He sold mainly dry goods, many in bulk. Anyone who wanted flour, oats or sugar could bring their own container and gets a measured amount from one of the giant hoppers on the shelf behind the counter. There'd been some opposition to this approach to start with, and Celia in particular had been concerned they'd be left with lots of stock they couldn't sell, but the scheme was a raging success and the 'Spotted in Coombesford' Facebook group was littered with suggestions, some practical, some less so, for what extra goods might be supplied in this way.

The shop also sold everyday essentials like milk from one of the local dairies, and artisan breads made in the Teign

Valley. There was a range of sweets for the children to buy on their way home from school, and an occasional oddity that caught Roger's eye during his visit to the wholesalers in Exeter. It was rumoured he was considering selling ice creams during the summer months, but Celia was trying to dissuade him as she believed the freezer would take up too much room.

To the right of the front door, the café was Celia's domain. Originally built as a bakery, it had a large room for customers, plus a decent sized kitchen. Behind the building was a large garden, used by visitors and staff alike in the summer.

For the next ten minutes Roger had a steady stream of customers, and by the time the rush had slackened, Simon Mountjoy was settled at the table in the window with coffee and one of Celia's currant buns. To Roger's surprise, Celia was sitting opposite him. And although he was too far away to hear what was being said, judging by the beaming smile on his wife's face she was enjoying their conversation. What on earth could that be about?

Roger didn't have to wait long to find out. Within a few minutes, Simon drained his coffee and jumped up. Throwing a wave in Roger's direction, which wasn't returned, he nodded at Celia and left. Celia came bustling over to Roger's counter.

"What did he want?" asked Roger. "After a favour, was he? That's the only time he's that friendly. I'm surprised he's got the cheek to show his face after all he's put us through."

"Oh, Roger, do give over." Celia put her hands on her ample hips and shook her head. "Actually, he's going to be doing us a favour, I reckon. You know that TV programme you like – the one where they look at old houses what's been done up? Well, they're making one at Mountjoy Manor. The film crew's coming this week."

"So what's that got to do with us, then?"

"Apparently they're staying in Newton Abbot, but Simon's going to point them in our direction at lunchtimes.

He wanted to warn me so I could have some extra baking done."

"Well," Roger said grudgingly, "I guess we can always do with extra footfall. I suppose he's not suggesting The Falls, as they'd all drink too much and not get any filming done in the afternoons. You know what these media types are like!"

"But that's not all!" Celia was obviously bursting to tell him more. "They want some additional footage from the village. And Simon's suggested they come in here. They'll do some background shots, maybe chat to you or me – and then interview Simon and Olga over a cup of coffee." She paused for breath and then clapped her hands together. "We're going to be famous, Roger. We're going to be on the telly!"

Roger wasn't at all sure he wanted to be on the telly himself, especially in a programme dedicated to Simon Mountjoy and that house of his. But he was delighted for Celia.

"Just so long as the film crew pay for their drinks and don't expect freebies, that's all!" he muttered as Celia scurried back to her customers.

CHAPTER 5: WEDNESDAY 3RD JULY

When Anthony Farsider parked in the driveway of Mountjoy Manor, the place was a hive of activity. A minibus bearing the name of a production company whose logo he regularly saw at the end of the credits on TV documentaries was parked on the hard-standing in front of the garage. A shiny black SUV was sitting next to it. Cables ran across the gravel and around the side of the house. In the distance, he could hear someone shouting. It all seemed so out of place in the grounds of this Devon manor house. Anthony sighed. He was getting too old for all this. He was so glad Marion had persuaded him to retire now he'd passed his seventieth birthday.

Hilda Reynolds opened the front door to him before he reached the top of the steps. Her face was devoid of makeup and her greying hair was in its customary bun. But she was wearing an elegant pants suit in cobalt blue, rather than her usual greys or blacks. The filming seemed to have got to her too.

"They've arrived, then?" he said.

"About six-thirty, I believe, Mr Farsider. They drove down last night. By the time I got here this morning, they were all set up and filming in the back garden." She peered around him at his car. "Oh, you've brought Millie! Doesn't she look wonderful?"

He looked back fondly at his immaculate 1950s Morris Minor Tourer, the cream roof and side panels folded back to show off the butter-coloured interior. He'd spent yesterday evening waxing and polishing her romaine green exterior to perfection.

"I'm taking her for a spin later; Marion and I are going to the coast for lunch. I thought I'd run her up here first to make sure everything's working well." He pointed to the other vehicles. "I hope she's not in the way there. I couldn't get into my usual spot today."

"She'll be fine," said Hilda. "And I'll keep an eye on her through the window."

"I hope Simon hasn't forgotten about our appointment, with everything else that's going on?"

"No, he's waiting for you in the office." She paused and pulled a face. "But I can't guarantee how long you'll be able to keep his attention. He's very excited about the whole thing."

It always amused Anthony to hear Simon's right-hand woman talk about him as though he was a young child. He suspected there might have been something going on between the two of them at some point. After all, they'd worked together for more than forty years. There had to be some reason she'd stuck with him that long. But on the one occasion he'd raised the subject with Simon, he'd been slapped down pretty quickly.

"Right, I'd better grab him while I can then," he said now. He tapped on the office door and walked straight in, as Hilda disappeared in the direction of the kitchen.

"Anthony, hello! Isn't this exciting? Did you see the crew out there?" Simon was standing at the open window, peering through the shrubbery from where the sounds of voices could be heard.

"Yes, yes. I'm looking forward to seeing the finished documentary." Anthony slipped off his jacket, hung it on the back of a chair, sat down at the conference table running along the back wall, and snapped open his briefcase. He pulled out a notebook and a manila folder. "Now, I know you're busy, Simon, so I'll make this quick."

Simon strolled over to join him, although his attention seemed to keep straying back to what was going on outside. Anthony tapped on the table with his nail and then opened his notebook and cleared his throat.

"I'm delighted to say the meetings in London went very well. Remarkably so, in fact. They're happy to accept our price and they're offering to keep all the staff on at their current salaries, even if that's above their norms."

"And what about our positions?"

"Well, as you know, I want to retire anyway. So they've offered me a three-month handover period then a very generous settlement package. And the same is on the table for you too."

"Me? But why would I want to give up work? Now this renovation's finished, I'm going to have more time on my hands, not less."

"Simon, we talked about this!" Anthony could feel the blood pounding in his temples, and paused to take a deep breath. "They want to bring their own management team in. That's non-negotiable."

"Well, it's non-negotiable with me too. I'm not being pushed out of my own company. I'd rather the deal didn't go ahead at all!"

Anthony was saved from responding to this as the door opened and Hilda walked in with coffee. She placed the tray at the end of the conference table and looked silently at the two men.

"It's all right, Hilda," said Simon irritably, "we'll serve ourselves. With a nod, she turned and left the room, pulling the door to behind her.

"That's another thing," said Anthony. "They've offered a very generous redundancy package for Hilda. I'm sure she'd love the chance for a bit of leisure time. Maybe travel a bit, even meet somebody?"

"Hilda," said Simon, looking up in surprise from the coffee pot. "Why on earth would Hilda want to take redundancy? She has no life outside of this company. And it's a bit late for her to start thinking about romance at her age, isn't it?" He shook his head. "I'm sorry, Anthony. I don't want to retire, so they're going to have to come up with another suggestion. But there's far too much going on at the moment. Let's talk about it next week, right?" He jumped up and picked up his coffee cup. "I'm going to take my drink outside to see how they're getting on. Why don't you join me?"

Pulling open the door, Simon stood back and gestured for his partner to precede him. In the hallway, Anthony caught movement from the corner of his eye, as someone disappeared around the corner into the kitchen.

CHAPTER 6: SATURDAY 6TH JULY

"Well, it looks like nearly everyone's here, even if they're not all enjoying themselves!" Charlie Jones threw herself down on the bench under the rose arch leading into the beer garden, blew her floppy dark fringe out of her eyes, and wrapped her arm around Annie's shoulders, pulling her towards her and giving her a squeeze.

Annie smiled at her wife and nodded.

"Yes, full house, certainly. And a beautiful day for it." She cocked her head to one side. "But why do you think they're not enjoying themselves? They all look fine to me."

"I'm not so sure. Just a feeling I've got." Charlie shrugged. "Maybe I'm wrong. Anyway, I think everyone's plates and glasses are full for now. Time for a quick breather."

"And Iris'll call us if anyone needs anything. Although she seems to be enjoying the chance to get out of the kitchen for a change and meet people."

"And if she doesn't, I'm sure her young assistant will! You know, Annie, I'm really proud of our Suzy. She's settled in so well. And she seems to be really popular with everyone, especially Iris."

"Just as well, considering how she follows her around," Annie said with a grin. "But it's good she's not afraid to pitch in if we need a hand collecting the empty plates – out here in the beer garden anyway. You know she told me the other day she wants to work in the pub trade," she used her fingers to mimic speech marks, "when she grows up."

"That probably won't last. And there's plenty of time for her to change her mind several times. She's only eight, after all. But Iris certainly seems to enjoy having her on hand to help today."

As the pair lounged in the sunshine, Charlie surveyed the crowded beer garden. Celia and Roger Richardson were sitting under one of the huge umbrellas, Roger in one of his trademark Hawaiian shirts over a pair of well-worn denim shorts. Celia, in a short-sleeved tee-shirt and floral print skirt, and with her bobbed blonde hair pushed into a hairband to keep it off her face, looked relaxed. The couple had closed up Cosy Corner early this afternoon, in order to enjoy the party.

"It's been a busy few days, what with all the film crew popping in and out all the time," Celia had said when they arrived. "We reckoned we deserved a couple of hours off."

The couple were chatting to animal lover and environmental activist, Pauline Wilson, who'd pulled her chair out of the shade and was rolling up her sleeves and the legs of her cargo pants to expose as much flesh as possible to the afternoon sun. The three spent quite a lot of time together and frequently popped in for a drink towards closing time. The fourth seat was taken by Pauline's mother, Elsie. Wearing a sun-hat, even in the shade, she took no part in the conversation, but gazed around her, smiling and waving to everyone who went past.

Anthony Farsider was standing near the bar with a group of locals. The only man present to be wearing a jacket, despite the heat, he was delivering an earnest critique of Exeter Chiefs' performance in the season just finished. There was much laughter and some barracking.

"I see Anthony's holding court," said Annie. "But he's not going to get much sympathy from that crowd. Football's much more their game than rugby."

Farsider may have been talking to the lads, but Charlie noticed his gaze repeatedly straying to a nearby table, where two middle-aged women sat. Occasionally, one of them would say something, and the other would nod and smile, or make some sort of reply, but most of the time, they just stared into space.

"Oh dear," said Annie, nodding her head towards the two women, "I see what you mean. It certainly doesn't look like those two are in the party spirit."

"I know Marion Farsider's quite shy," said Charlie. "In fact, I think this is only the second time I've seen her in here this year. But Hilda Reynolds is usually much friendlier than that. I wonder what's got into her?"

"Well, normally when she's in here, she doesn't have the boss's wife and her personal trainer sitting close by, does she? Although for all the attention those two are paying anyone else, they might as well not be here."

Charlie looked across at where the younger couple were stretched out on loungers, deep in conversation, ignoring everyone else. Nathan Williams was conservatively dressed in black shorts and running shoes. His skin-tight vest did nothing to hide his well-toned muscles. By contrast Olga Mountjoy, with the high cheekbones betraying her Slavic ancestry, was expensively and scantily clothed in a silky cropped top and shorts. Her long legs were tanned and her feet were encased in white leather mules decorated with rhinestones.

Charlie jumped, as Annie put a hand on her arm and gently pinched her.

"Down, girl," she said with a grin. Then she stood and held her hand. "Come on; time to get back to work. Iris and Suzy will think we've run off and left them to it."

For the next hour, the pair and Iris Murphy, their chef, were kept busy ferrying food from the kitchen to the plates held out by hungry guests; or refilling glasses. Eight-year-old Suzy McLeod-Jones, blonde hair in pigtails and a huge chef's apron wrapped around her tiny frame, buzzed about collecting dirty plates. At five o'clock, Charlie climbed onto one of the benches and tapped on her glass for silence. There was a groan from one of the football fans, followed by shushing from his friends and a smattering of applause.

"It's okay, folks, I'm only going to take a minute of your time," she said. "I just want to thank you all for coming along today to help us celebrate our first anniversary."

"Well, the free food helped," called out the irrepressible youth in the corner.

Charlie acknowledged the jibe with a grin before resuming her speech. "You've all made us feel so welcome here in Coombesford. Annie and I are really enjoying running The Falls." She glanced across to the back of the crowd, where their daughter was jumping up and down, waving her arm in the air. "And Suzy wants you to know she's having a great time too. I hope you've all noticed our guest waitress this afternoon."

"Well done, Suzy," called out someone from the crowd.

"Make sure they pay you a decent wage," came another voice.

Just then Iris appeared from the kitchen, carrying a huge cake on a wooden platter.

"As you can see," said Charlie, "our chef's really gone to town on the baking today. So let's all raise our glasses to Coombesford and The Falls. Then I'll shut up and we'll all have a piece of cake."

"Coombesford." "The Falls." "Charlie and Annie." "Suzy, the best waitress in Devon." As the toasts echoed around the beer garden, someone started to applaud. And soon, everyone was clapping and cheering. Charlie held out her hands to Annie and Suzy, and the three of them stood together, beaming at their customers, many of whom were rapidly becoming friends as well.

"I'm so sorry I'm late. Have I missed everything?" Charlie spun around as a voice behind her made her jump.

CHAPTER 7

Simon Mountjoy wore smartly-pressed chinos and a rugby shirt bearing the colours of the England team. A pale mauve sweater was loosely knotted around his neck. His brown loafers were highly polished. He was the nearest thing Coombesford had to a squire – and Charlie knew he liked to play the part. She smiled and shook her head.

"No, Simon, you're fine. You've missed my speech and the toasts, but we're just about to cut the cake and there's plenty of food left in the kitchen. Come and get a drink – everything's on the house today."

"I've been filming all day and lost track of the time," he explained as he took a deep gulp from a glass of red wine. "I sometimes think this documentary is a bigger project than the restoration itself!"

Charlie knew all about the documentary. It was the talk of the village. The thirteen-year project to restore Mountjoy Manor had been a labour of love, or an expensive folly, depending on who was talking. But there was general agreement the fifteenth-century property on the edge of the village was looking a world away from the dilapidated wreck Simon had bought when he moved back to Devon after a successful career in an electronics company. And now, it was being immortalised in a television documentary series on architectural restoration.

"Will the film crew be joining us, Simon?" she asked. "They'd be more than welcome. They've brought a fair bit of trade to us and the café this week."

"Yes, they'll be along in a little while. They're just packing up for the day. There's a bit more to do tomorrow morning, then they're done."

There was a roar of laughter from the sports fans by the bar. Charlie nodded towards them.

"Probably just as well the cameras won't be rolling tonight."

Charlie watched from the sideline as Simon wandered around, working the crowd. He chatted with Celia Richardson who laughed at one of his jokes. Roger Richardson and Pauline Wilson appeared to take no part in the conversation and both glowered after Simon as he moved on. His casual wave to Anthony Farsider was acknowledged with a slight nod.

Finally, he stopped at the table where Hilda Reynolds and Marion Farsider were sitting. His executive assistant became more animated than she'd been all afternoon, and although Charlie was too far away to hear what was said, her gesture was obvious. As Simon took a seat, Marion Farsider gave the pair a stiff smile, then got up and walked away. Her husband watched her as he continued to chat to his friends.

"Now that's strange," said Charlie to Iris, who'd just arrived back from the kitchen with a pile of plates and a tray of sliced cake.

"What's strange, Charlie?"

"Well, Simon's made a point of chatting to, or acknowledging virtually everyone here, apart from his own wife and that trainer chap of hers."

Iris sniffed. "Well, I did hear it's not exactly a marriage made in heaven." She turned on her heel, and strode off towards the kitchen.

Not that Olga Mountjoy seemed to mind, Charlie thought. The Ukrainian woman had barely glanced up when her husband arrived. She was still deep in conversation with her companion. Charlie picked up a tray and wandered through the crowd.

"It's looking very good, Hilda," Simon was saying as Charlie reached their table. He was holding his mobile in front of them and from the tinny sounds issuing from it, he was running a video. "I think you'll be impressed with the result. And it's certainly going to put Mountjoy Manor on the map." He rubbed his hands together. "We'll have tours coming from all over Devon by the time we've finished; maybe even further." He turned and looked over his shoulder. "Olga, come and look at this. Your home's going to be famous."

"Oh, Simon darling, I'm too comfortable to move," was the heavily accented reply. "Pass the phone over here." Her husband obliged and, as Charlie watched, Olga and Nathan huddled over the small screen.

"This is only the background stuff," Simon went on. "How I raised the money to buy the house in the first place and so on. And a bit about getting the gong, services to industry, innovation, that sort of thing. But wait until you see the footage they've taken of the grounds and the interior."

As the evening wore on, the crowd remained as large as ever, with several of the regulars settled in for the night. Charlie had wanted to book an Exeter-based sixties tribute band to round off the event. Suzy had suggested they try to book Muse! But Annie had won the day and, as they listened to the gentle sounds of a local folk band, Charlie had to admit Annie had been right. She must remember to tell her that at some point, but maybe later on, rather than right now. First she needed to top up the ice box. The white wine was starting to warm up.

"I don't know how you can walk around here so smugly, after what you did to my charity!" The harsh words cut across the night, and as Charlie turned the corner, she came across Pauline Wilson standing facing Simon Mountjoy, with her hands on her hips. The woman was swaying ever so slightly.

"You've been drinking again, Pauline. Why don't you go and sleep it off?" Simon stepped around her and, with a smile and a raised eyebrow at Charlie, walked back towards his table. Pauline exhaled sharply and leaned back against the wall.

"Are you okay, Pauline?" asked Charlie. The other woman jumped and put her hand to her chest.

"Oh, Charlie, you made me jump. I didn't see you there." She nodded her head. "Yes, I'm fine. It's just that man makes me so mad! He swans around like he owns the place…" She stopped and grimaced. "Maybe he's right. Maybe I should go home. Mum must be ready for her bed by now." But as she walked unsteadily back towards her table, she turned back to Charlie and held up a finger. "But you mark my words. One day, someone's going to give that man what's coming to him. And when they do, I'll be right there on the sideline, cheering them on."

CHAPTER 8: SUNDAY 7TH JULY

Simon waited until the guests were all seated then sat down at the head of the table. They'd strolled around the garden sipping their pre-lunch drinks, the noisy chatter suggesting a job well done, after four long days of interviews and filming. But the midday sun burned in the cloudless sky and everyone had seemed happy to move under the umbrellas on the patio when Hilda called them to eat.

Simon had told her to keep it simple, and as usual she'd done exactly what was required. The folks at the deli in Chudleigh had provided a whole poached salmon, thinly sliced gammon and turkey, plus huge bowls of salad. Baskets of crusty bread and dishes of local butter completed the spread.

"Dig in," called Simon over the hubbub. "No standing on ceremony here!"

He sat back in his chair and watched as the guests took him at his word. The director, Aggie, in her mid-thirties and a bundle of energy, sat on his left. He'd found himself drawn to her from the start, but even he drew the line at playing around in his own backyard, with his wife so close by. Although he wasn't sure whether Olga would care or not. Still, maybe there'd be an opportunity to extend their relationship during the post-production stages. He must remember to suggest a meeting in London before the crew departed later on.

Aggie's assistant, Paul, sat next to her, as he had throughout the visit. He looked to be barely out of short trousers, although Simon acknowledged most people looked young by the time you reached your late sixties.

Next to Paul sat Anthony Farsider. Simon knew his business partner was not best pleased with him at the moment, and he hoped some socialising would help. He'd wanted to sort it out yesterday, but Anthony had spent most of the evening talking sport and seemed to be avoiding him. Maybe they could talk once the film crew left. Marian Farsider sat to Simon's right, but for all the conversation he'd got out of her so far, the seat might as well be empty.

The cameraman, a New Zealander called Mike, had told Simon he was taking a break from backpacking around the world and earning some money to continue his travels. Sitting the other side of Anthony, he was deep in conversation with Olga, at the foot of the table, and Nathan, inevitably on her left. Olga was in her element, Simon thought, as the two young men roared with laughter at something she said.

The remaining places at the table, between Nathan and Marion, were taken up by the two male technicians. Simon hadn't even learned their names in the five days they'd been there. They spent most of the time in the background making unintelligible comments that sounded like a different language to him. Even now, they were discussing the finer points of lighting and sound, and seemed quite happy left on their own. So much the better. Simon could concentrate on Aggie.

Through the glass doors into the kitchen, Simon could see Hilda chatting with the caterer. He'd invited her to join them for lunch, as he always did, but as was so often the case, she'd declined. No doubt she'd get herself something from the leftovers when the rest of them had finished.

By the time the main dishes were cleared away, to be

replaced by tureens of fresh fruit and a magnificent pavlova for anyone not concerned about the calories, Simon was feeling very mellow indeed. And looking around the table, he saw he wasn't the only one.

"You really are so lucky to have this wonderful house," gushed Aggie. "We've seen some great properties doing this show over the years, but I think this might be one of my favourites. Just the right blend of authenticity and luxury. And that view!" She waved her arm around to encompass the sloping gardens, the valley and the distant moors.

"Yes, it's not bad, is it?" he replied. "Although I'm not sure luck had a lot to do with it. Shrewd investment and hard work would be more like it. I've always prided myself on being able to spot a trend before the next guy. And it's paid off big time on a couple of occasions."

"Like the cable tidy you talked about in your interview? The one that got you your innovation award? Such a simple idea; makes you wonder why no-one else thought about it first?"

"Well, it's common sense really, and you know what they say about common sense. But it was really a case of right time, right place. And grabbing an opportunity when it presented itself." Sensing the rest of the table had gone quiet, and not wanting to ruin the atmosphere, Simon stood and picked up the nearest wine bottle. "Right, who needs a top-up?"

At that moment, he spied a movement out of the corner of his eye. Someone had walked around the side of the house and was standing at the bottom of the slope by the pool room, staring up at him.

"It's the chef from The Falls," Olga drawled. "What does she want? They're not doing the catering, are they, Simon?"

Everyone turned to watch as the woman walked up towards them. She was somewhere in her thirties, her long chestnut hair loose and flowing over her bare shoulders. She wore faded denim jeans and a strappy top, and her tanned arms and freckled face suggested she was used to being outside. A delicate cascade of flowers was tattooed across her right shoulder and down her arm. Simon thought she looked magnificent. He wondered once more where he'd seen her before. At the barbecue the previous day, he'd thought she looked familiar; now he was even more sure.

"Hello. It's Iris, isn't it? From The Falls?" he said. "We're just finishing lunch. Would you like to join us for a drink, or coffee?"

"I need to talk to you, Simon," she said brusquely. "In private!"

"Well, really!" Olga jumped to her feet. "Can't you see we've got guests!"

But Simon held up his hand to silence his wife.

"It's okay, Olga. I'll deal with this." Then, turning to Iris, he pointed towards the house. "Let's go into my office. We can talk there." He had no idea what the woman wanted, but he was fairly sure he wouldn't want to have the conversation in front of guests, especially not a film crew.

CHAPTER 9

As Simon led Iris Murphy through the house towards his office, Hilda Reynolds watched and bit her lip. She'd known Iris was going to arrive some time today, but hadn't been sure when. She'd begged her to approach the problem differently, but the other woman was adamant. She didn't want to make a formal appointment; she wanted to catch Simon unawares.

"That's the best way to get an honest answer out of the man," she'd insisted when they'd talked at the barbecue the previous day. "If he has time to prepare, he'll have his story sorted out. And I don't want to give him the chance to do that."

Hilda knew she should have warned her boss. That's where her main loyalties should lie. But there were other considerations. And after the conversation she'd heard between Simon and Anthony, things were no longer clear cut. She bit her lip as she chided herself. Her mother always told her you never heard anything good by eavesdropping; and it looked as if she'd been proved right again. But maybe it was just as well to know what Simon thought about her. Maybe it was finally time she started thinking about herself rather than him.

Hilda glanced out at the patio. Everyone else seemed to

have gone back to their conversations. The sunshine, and an excess of food and wine, apparently made them incurious about what was going on with their host. All except Olga, that was. She was perched on the edge of her chair, glaring in the direction of the house. When Nathan leaned forward and tried to speak to her she brushed him aside with an impatient flick of her hand. He shrugged and raised his eyebrows before carrying on chatting to Mike the cameraman.

Hilda wondered how long it would be before Olga lost patience and went in search of her husband and his unexpected visitor. She gave it ten minutes tops.

In fact, it was eight minutes exactly before Olga jumped up, sending her chair flying. Everyone stopped talking at the sudden crash.

"Please, carry on chatting and do help yourselves to more wine," said Olga through what sounded to Hilda like gritted teeth. "I'll just go and see how the staff are getting on with the coffee." She paused and gave an elegant little shrug. "And maybe see what's keeping your host."

Hilda looked around the kitchen, empty now the caterers had headed home, promising to return in the morning for the empty dishes. Olga was checking on the staff, was she? That would be her, then. She turned to the coffee machine and checked it was switched on. Presumably, she'd be expected to take the individual orders too.

"Ah, Hilda, there you are." The Ukrainian accent was as grating as ever. "Who is that woman? And why does she need to talk to Simon today?"

"I have no idea, Olga. Maybe you should ask him?" She tried to keep the disdain out of her voice, but suspected she might not quite have succeeded.

When they'd first met, Simon's second wife had suggested Hilda call her Mrs Mountjoy, and much as it would have rankled, Hilda would have done so, had Simon not scotched the idea.

"Don't be silly, darling," he'd said. "Hilda's been with

me more than thirty years. She's part of the family!"

Now, as the other woman glared at her, Hilda reflected she might be part of Simon's family, but she doubted if she would ever be a welcome member of Olga's.

The sound of raised voices broke the moment. Olga strode into the hallway. Hilda followed, and found her staring at the closed door leading to the office. Through the solid oak, it was difficult to hear what was being said, but Simon and Iris appeared to be shouting both at once.

"This is ridiculous," fumed Olga, hands on hips and rhinestone-decorated toe tapping on the highly polished parquet flooring. "We have guests." She turned and pointed at Hilda. "Go in and stop this."

"But…"

"It's your job to make Simon's life easy, isn't?" Hilda wasn't sure that was quite how she would write her job description, but decided this wasn't the time to argue. Olga continued, "If you don't go in there right now, I'm going to get Simon to fire you!"

Good luck with that, lady, thought Hilda. She'd outlasted one wife and numerous girlfriends over the years. She didn't think wife number two was going to be any different.

At that moment the office door was wrenched open, slamming backwards into the wall, as Iris Murphy charged out into the hall, narrowly avoiding crashing into Olga. Her face was bright red and tears were spilling down her cheeks. Simon stood framed in the doorway, mouth open, shock etched on his face.

Hilda stepped forward, her arms reaching out, but Iris just shook her head.

"Not now, Hilda," she said. Then as she reached the front door, she turned and yelled at Simon. "I don't know why I came. You'll never change. You killed her! And I'm going to make sure you pay!"

CHAPTER 10

Following the disruption of Iris Murphy's visit, the lunch party had broken up fairly quickly. The film crew were picked up by their driver in the company minibus. Aggie, who had stuck to sparkling water throughout lunch, climbed into her SUV, accompanied by her assistant Paul. Both vehicles headed for the motorway and a long journey back to London, amid much waving and promises to be in touch soon.

Anthony attempted to talk to Simon, but found him moody and unresponsive. Olga had disappeared and Nathan, the only other one not to have been drinking heavily, announced he was off for a swim. Marion Farsider complained of a headache, so Anthony admitted defeat and agreed to walk her home, telling Simon he would be back later that evening.

"We really have to sort this thing out today, Simon," was his parting comment. "We can't hang around any longer."

Now, as he walked back up the drive, he heard the church clock strike seven. The heat of the afternoon was starting to die down, but it was still very pleasant. If only he didn't have this problem to sort out, he could quite enjoy his evening stroll. Maybe once he'd finished talking to Simon, he'd loop round through the lanes and call into The

Falls for a pint. The beer garden should be quiet at this time on a Sunday evening.

Ringing the doorbell had no effect. He wasn't really surprised. No doubt the ever-efficient Hilda would have left for her Exeter apartment by now. So, as he had done so many times before, Anthony headed around the side of the house, through the shrubbery and past the pool room. Glancing up at the patio, he spotted Olga and Nathan relaxing with mugs of coffee. Their heads were close together and they didn't notice Anthony until he coughed discreetly.

"Oh, hello, Anthony," called Olga. "Simon's not here, I'm afraid."

"Well, where is he? I told him I was coming back this evening. It's imperative I talk to him."

Olga pulled a face and shrugged.

"No idea. He's hardly said a word since that woman's performance this afternoon. We're supposed to be meeting friends down in Teignmouth at eight, but if he doesn't get back soon, it's not going to be worth driving down there."

"You could try the site office," said Nathan. "I saw him heading up the drive earlier on and he was wearing his work boots."

The site office was located on a new housing development on the other side of the village. Farsider-Mountjoy Developments Ltd was the principal contractor and the pair had set up a small Portacabin to use for site meetings.

"Very well. I'll stroll across there," Anthony said. "I was heading that way later anyway." He began to walk away, then stopped and turned back. "But if he comes back in the meantime, please tell him to ring me. I have to talk to him tonight. I don't care how late it is."

"Yes, yes, of course we will," said Olga, before resuming her conversation with Nathan. Anthony grunted to himself as he set off once more. Somehow, he suspected those two would barely notice if poor Simon returned or not.

In the gloom, Anthony thought the site office was empty to begin with, until he switched on the light and saw the figure slumped behind the desk. Simon didn't look well at all and Anthony suspected he'd carried on drinking after the lunch party had finished, although his partner denied it vigorously. Sitting down in the visitor's chair in front of the desk, Anthony cleared his throat.

"Now listen, Simon, I know you don't want to talk about this, but we need to come to a decision if we're not going to lose the deal altogether."

Simon looked up and shook his head.

"Not this again, Anthony. I told you, I don't want to retire. And if that's a deal breaker, then so be it."

"But why not? It's a good deal; a great deal, in fact. And let's face it, neither of us is getting any younger!"

"Rubbish. We've got years left in us yet. And we built this company up together. Why do you want to get rid of it now? There's all those new houses the government's pushing for, especially down here. We stand to make a packet."

Anthony stared at his partner in silence for a few moments. He was going to have to tell him, that was plain. Marion had begged him to keep it secret for as long as possible. But without sharing the new situation with Simon, there didn't seem any way of getting him to change his mind.

"Look," he said eventually, "what I'm going to tell you has to stay between us for the moment…"

Shockingly, when he finished talking, it was as though he'd said nothing of import at all. Simon just shook his head, and said he couldn't think about it at that moment.

"We'll talk tomorrow, Anthony. I promise." And with that, he jumped up and hurried out of the office. Through the open doorway, Anthony watched him plough his way through the muddy ground, head down and hands in his pockets. At the gate to the site, he turned left and headed in the direction of Mountjoy Manor and home.

CHAPTER 11: MONDAY 8TH JULY

The sun shining through the open curtains woke Charlie just before five, and she lay there, luxuriating in her life and how there was nowhere else she'd rather be, for half an hour before slipping into the en suite for a quick shower. Annie was still sound asleep and there was no movement from Suzy's room. It was already warm and the scorching summer's day promised by the weather forecaster looked as if it was going to materialise. Charlie quietly closed the door behind her and strolled across the lawn and through the beer garden. She paused at the back door of The Falls and looked across at the building where her little family was sleeping. One of the first things they'd done when they moved to Devon, was to have the huge downstairs room and tiny bathroom in The Folly converted into two en-suite rooms. The upstairs lounge area they'd left as it was.

Charlie walked along the passageway, past the stairs to the guest bedrooms, and pushed open the door into the bar-cum-restaurant. She let the door swing gently shut behind her. It was just past six in the morning and although she was wide awake, she knew several of the guests would be nowhere near stirring yet.

The party on Saturday had been proof enough, but Charlie still had to pinch herself occasionally to be sure she wasn't dreaming. They'd done it! Escaped from London, from the daily commute she'd grown to hate, from the noise and the dirt of the South East. Suzy had settled in well at the local primary school, and she and Annie had been made very welcome by most of the villagers. There was the occasional comment or disapproving look, but hey, you got that anywhere.

Charlie hummed to herself as she pottered around the bar. Sunday evening had been quiet. She suspected many of the regulars were still recovering from the previous day's party. She and Annie had cleared up all the dirty glasses within twenty minutes of closing time, before heading across the garden to their room. All Charlie had to do now was unpack the dishwasher and put the glasses back on the shelves. She flicked the switch on the coffee machine and checked the water heater was on. Then she crossed the bar and surveyed the dining area, where three tables were set for breakfast. Not bad for a Monday morning during term time. They were hoping for a full house once the schools broke up and the summer holidays kicked in, but they were doing fine as it was.

The tables were scrubbed pine with matching chairs. They'd decided against tablecloths, saving both costs and the environment by reducing their laundry bill, but had splashed out on some pretty vintage china tea services at the various second-hand shops and stalls in Newton Abbot, Totnes and Teignmouth. And on each table there was a little vase of real flowers. That was Suzy's job, keeping the vases full, and she'd shown great aptitude for it. The Falls had well-stocked borders and rockeries, edging the semi-formal beer garden plus an area beyond The Folly, which ran down to the stream and had been left to run wild. Suzy had explored every inch of the grounds and discovered numerous flowers and shrubs with suitable foliage. This time last year, Charlie and Annie had wondered whether she'd be able to keep it up throughout the winter as well, but she had. They were finding their young daughter to be very resourceful. *Mind you,* thought Charlie, *some of those vases look a little sad this morning.* After her busy day on Saturday, Suzy had been flaked out for most of Sunday.

Charlie glanced at her watch. Time to take the butter and milk out of the fridge and distribute on each table. As she was carrying the tray full of dishes and milk jugs across from the kitchen to the dining area, she heard footsteps in the passage and Annie pushed her way through the door. She looked fresh and cool in a sleeveless sun dress that showed off the creamy skin on her arms, just starting to settle into a slight tan. The large pink flowers around the hem matched exactly the colour of her cropped hair. Over the years, Annie had toned it down from the deep purple she'd been dying it when they first met, but her hair colour was still the most outstanding feature of this otherwise quiet, gentle woman. Charlie grinned at her and blew her a kiss. She felt lucky all over again.

The pair worked side by side getting everything ready, and by twenty past seven, they'd run out of things to do. Annie looked around the bar and then squeezed Charlie's arm.

"We're so lucky," she said. "I'm really glad you persuaded me to come and see this place."

"Yes, definitely one of my better ideas, wasn't it?" Charlie rubbed her hands together. "Right, I've just got time to move that crate of empties outside before the ravening hordes arrive."

"Right. There's a delivery due later this morning, isn't there?"

"And I'll pop down to the meadow and grab a bunch of stuff to refresh those vases while I'm at it. Suzy didn't get around to it yesterday."

She picked up a crate of empty beer bottles and walked through the rear of the bar and down the passageway to the back door. To one side was a paved area, accessed from the driveway at the side of the building, where all deliveries were made. Dropping the crate next to the others awaiting collection, she crossed the beer garden and headed downhill towards the stream.

Reaching up to pluck some spikes of buddleia from a large bush, she glanced towards the stream, as something caught her eye.

CHAPTER 12

Within minutes, Charlie was joined by a first responder on a motorbike. She knew him by sight; Dave something or other. He lived in one of the houses on the new estate and ate in the bar most Wednesdays when his wife was out at her book club. He quickly confirmed they were dealing with a dead body and called the ambulance service to notify them there was no hurry as the 'patient' was not going anywhere.

"The police will need to start their investigation before we can move the body," he said. He rang off and turned to Charlie. "Did you touch anything?" Charlie shook her head. "It's Simon Mountjoy," he went on. "Him that owns the big house they've just finished renovating."

"Yes, I know Simon," said Charlie. "In fact, he was here for our anniversary party on Saturday evening. It looks like he fell in further upstream and got carried over the waterfall. Maybe he had a heart attack. Or a stroke?"

Dave pursed his lips and shook his head.

"Well, I'm no expert, but it looks more like a suspicious death to me." He pointed to the bruises on Simon's face. "Those will have come when he went over the falls, but that wound on the side of his head looks like he's been hit more than once in the same place." He stepped back from the edge of the water. "You're going to have to keep this area secure for the moment. It's probably a crime scene."

"That's not a problem; no-one comes down here but us. But who'd want to hurt Simon? He seemed so popular."

"That's up to the police," said Dave. "They'll start by interviewing you and your staff; then they'll want to talk to the rest of the villagers." He grinned. "But they'll not be short of suspects in this case. Popular? Not our Mr Mountjoy, I'm afraid. Not a popular man at all!"

By the time the police had finished their initial investigation of the scene and arranged for the body to be taken away, it was after two in the afternoon. The area around the stream was taped off and everyone warned to keep away from it. Charlie had been tied up talking to the police for much of the time, while Annie had covered for her not only at breakfast but also for the lunchtime trade. News of the discovery of a body hadn't yet spread widely and the delivery driver due to collect the empties and top up their supply of bottled beers had arrived late morning as arranged. Charlie just hoped they'd ordered enough.

"I suspect we'll have a full house tonight once the news gets out," she said to Annie as they strolled across the green.

"Well, if the beer runs out, they'll just have to drink wine or cider," said Annie, practical as ever.

The couple had decided to grab a late lunch in Cosy Corner. The Falls was closed in the afternoons and neither of them really fancied staying put, given what was going on there at the moment.

The café's counter was a relatively small one flanked by glass cases displaying the range of goodies on sale each day. There wasn't a huge choice – a couple of cakes and two or three types of cookies, plus Celia's famous pasties, which sold out rapidly every lunchtime and whose tantalizing aroma was the first thing people noticed when they walked through the door. Folks had suggested Celia expand into salads and baked potatoes, but she always said she was much happier being 'the best place in the area for coffee and cake' rather than trying to increase her range and being mediocre at everything as a result.

The café seated around twenty, at square tables. The Richardsons had scoured junk shops in the region for nice old tables and chairs that could be restored and added to the stock. Drinks were served in mismatched, but beautiful, old-fashioned china cups and saucers. In fact, it had been this which encouraged Charlie and Annie to take a similar approach in the pub. Cakes were similarly served on china plates. Celia's parents, the previous owners, had used paper napkins for speed and convenience, but Celia had gone back to using cotton ones. She'd once told Charlie and Annie it was because the environmental lobby was pushing for all single use items to be phased out, but they suspected she was secretly much happier with tables set with gingham cloths and napkins.

Cosy Corner was quiet. The lunchtime rush was over and the post school-run crowd had yet to appear. Charlie and Annie took a table in the back of the room close to the counter, and ordered one pasty between them, followed by a slice of walnut sponge. Charlie had black coffee, while Annie opted for mint tea.

"You're in luck, me lovelies," Celia said, as she bustled around behind the counter sorting out their order. "We've been quite busy today, but I've got one pasty left. Roger had his eye on it, but he can have a bit of cake with his afternoon tea instead."

A single customer in the grocery side finished their purchases, paid up and left. Even before the ding of the doorbell had faded away, Roger darted out from behind his counter and strode across to their table.

"Is it true?" he demanded. Charlie's heart sank and she glanced across at Annie, exhaling sharply.

"Is what true, Roger?" she asked, knowing full well what he was going to say, but unprepared for just how forcefully he was going to express it.

"Is it true there's a body been found below the waterfall?

And it's that bugger Simon Mountjoy?"

"Well, I'm not sure we're supposed to say anything," said Annie. "The police said they'll be issuing a statement later today. We need to wait for that-"

But Roger cut across her.

"—this is a small village, Annie. Everyone knows what's going on, as soon as it happens. And I heard Simon Mountjoy was found dead behind your pub this morning. So is it true or not?"

Charlie shrugged at Annie and then nodded her head.

"Yes, Roger, I'm afraid it's true," she said. Then she sat back in amazement as Roger began slowly to grin.

Celia shot out from behind the counter and grabbed her husband by the arm.

"Roger Richardson, you show some respect right now," she said. And as the door pinged once more, she gave him a little push. "You get back over there this minute and leave these folks in peace to eat their lunch. You've got a customer to serve."

She smiled an apology at Charlie and Annie, then returned to her own counter. But throughout the rest of their lunch, they heard Roger humming to himself. And each time they caught his eye, he grinned at them and winked.

CHAPTER 13

Detective Chief Inspector Andrea Harolds and Detective Sergeant Pete Smith spent their afternoon calling on the grieving widow.

"What do we know about this place, Pete?" asked the DCI as they walked up the hill leading from Fore Street to Mountjoy Manor. The sergeant pulled out his notebook and gave a nervous cough.

"Well, according to its website, Mountjoy Manor was originally built in the late 1400s, was renovated and adapted over the next four hundred years before falling into considerable disrepair in the twentieth century. It was the house Simon Mountjoy was brought up in, but his mother sold it in the 1970s. There were a couple of attempts to turn it into a business, one as a boutique hotel and the other as a retreat for writers, but both ran out of money and the place had been deserted for the best part of twenty years before Mountjoy bought it back in 2006." He closed his notebook and looked delighted with himself, as though he'd been able to answer a difficult question put to him by defence counsel in the witness box.

"Well, it doesn't look in disrepair now," was Harolds' only comment. The detectives paused as they reached the entrance to the property. The towering wrought iron gates were closed and Smith pressed a bell nearly hidden by ivy on one of the stone gate posts. After a brief pause, the gates swung open. The house appeared to have three storeys, constructed of Devon stone in different shades of greys and browns, with a heavily decorated porch leading up three steps to a solid dark-stained oak front door. The gravelled driveway was hemmed in with neatly tended flowerbeds and shrubberies. There was an air of prosperity and self-satisfaction about the place. They climbed the steps and Smith raised the ornate knocker and rapped on the oak panel.

The front door was opened by a middle-aged woman in a black trouser suit and white silk blouse. Her eyes were rimmed red and puffy. Harolds held out her hand.

"Mrs Mountjoy, I'm DCI Andrea Harolds. I'm really sorry to bother you at this terrible time, but we need to ask you a few questions."

"No, ma'am," Smith jumped in, "this is Miss Hilda Reynolds, Mr Mountjoy's executive assistant."

The woman opened her mouth to speak, but her eyes welled with tears and she shook her head, pointing down the hallway to the back of the house.'

"You'll find Mrs Mountjoy on the terrace," the woman managed to gasp before tears overwhelmed her once more and she turned away and disappeared rapidly into a room to the right of the hallway. Before the door closed, Harolds had time to glimpse desks, computers and a large laser printer.

"He used to run his business from here too," Smith said.

The front door led into an equally impressive entrance hall. There was a carved stone fireplace on the right-hand wall, past the door through which Hilda Reynolds had vanished.

"That's constructed in Dartmoor granite," said Smith. The DCI suspected he hoped his extensive knowledge of the house would make up for not briefing her sufficiently on its residents. "The carving over the mantelpiece was described as the ancient Mountjoy family crest," Smith continued, "although I did a bit of research and it's more likely the deceased got the design and a 'certificate of authenticity' off the internet after he bought the house."

"Thank you, Smith. I think that will do for the background on the house," said Harolds dryly. "As we seem to have been abandoned, we'd better make our way out to the terrace."

They walked down the passageway and into a large kitchen-dining area. To their left was a fitted kitchen of huge proportions, obviously hand-made and customised to taste. In the centre of the room was a small round wooden table with four chairs, ideal for informal dining. And to their right, three large squashy sofas around a glass coffee table provided a relaxation area.

In the corner, an open doorway revealed a flight of stairs leading downward. Harolds heard the sound of splashing.

"It's in the old cellars," said Smith. "You can't see it from the front, but the house is actually four storeys in all."

The back wall, running across the whole width of the house, was made of glass. It opened out onto a patio area housing a huge table and chairs. A folded umbrella and stand stood in one corner. The garden sloped away from the patio, and looked to be a mix of carefully tended beds and cottage garden type borders overflowing with shrubs. Beyond the fence at the bottom of the slope, the Haldon hills rose into the distance. The tiny valley looked secluded and undisturbed by modern life.

The glass doors to the garden were pushed back and a woman sat at the table on the terrace, staring out across the garden.

"Mrs Mountjoy," Smith called out. "Can we come through? The Detective Chief Inspector needs to talk to you."

The newly-widowed woman turned and nodded.

Close to, Harolds realised Olga Mountjoy was not quite as young as she appeared from a distance. There were a few

47

lines at her mouth and around her eyes. But her figure was superb, and when she pushed the sleeves of her robe up above her elbows, there was not a sign of her developing bat-wings. The woman from Ukraine, who had ended up married to the biggest businessman in the village, was wearing well for her age, the DCI acknowledged a trifle enviously.

"How can I help you, detectives?"

Harolds expressed her condolences and explained they needed to ask some questions. Olga shrugged and reached into her pocket for cigarettes and a lighter. As she blew out a long stream of smoke through her nose she nodded to Harolds to continue. Her responses were straightforward and given without hesitation. She'd last seen her husband late on Sunday afternoon, after their guests had left. He'd been sitting here on the terrace, brooding over something. She'd gone up to her room for a shawl and when she came back down, he'd gone. Nathan had seen him go, and said Simon was carrying his work boots, so she assumed he was going to the site office. Yes, that was quite usual. No, she hadn't realised he'd had an accident. She'd gone to bed early with a headache, taken a couple of sleeping pills and not woken until ten this morning when Hilda Reynolds knocked on her bedroom door to tell her the police were downstairs. No, she couldn't suggest why her husband had been anywhere near the stream. His walks were usually around the lanes leading out of the village.

"Mrs Mountjoy," Harolds said, "I'm afraid we now believe your husband's death was no accident. While most of his injuries were consistent with going over the waterfall, there were signs he was attacked first. And we expect the post-mortem to confirm he was dead before he entered the water. We're treating this as a murder investigation."

"Oh," said Olga. "Thank you for telling me." And that was it. No further reaction. Harolds couldn't work out whether she was stunned or didn't care.

"Can you think of anyone who might want to harm your

husband, Mrs Mountjoy?" asked Smith.

"Not really. I know he wasn't very popular in the village. Although I don't see why. He brought a lot of work and income to this place." She paused and pulled a face. "Of course, you might want to ask that woman from the pub what their row was all about," she finished, stubbing her cigarette out in a cut glass ashtray.

"Which woman would that be, Mrs Mountjoy? And what row?"

"The one that works in the kitchen." She bit her lip and put her head on one side. "Iris, her name is, Iris Murphy. She was up here yesterday afternoon, demanding to speak to Simon. He took her into the office to talk, and they were in there for ages. We had guests; it was so embarrassing. I went to look for him in the end. And as I got to the hall, I heard shouting. Then the door to the office flew open, and she raged out, heading for the front door. She was in such a temper, she nearly knocked me over as she ran past."

"And did you ask your husband what the argument had been about?"

"No, there wasn't time. I just wanted him to come back to our guests. I was going to ask him later. But now, I think maybe it might have been linked, if he was killed just a few hours later. She accused him of being responsible for someone's death and threatened him. Said she'd make him pay!"

As Harolds and Smith stood to take their leave, Olga yawned, stretched her arms above her head and gave a sigh. Then she went back to staring at the horizon.

"Well, what did you think of that?" Harolds asked as they walked back down the hill towards the green and the centre of the village.

"Difficult to judge really. She's a bit of a cold fish; but I guess she's just had a hell of a shock. She's probably trying to work out what's going to happen to her now her meal ticket's dead."

'True, but I was talking about her description of

Mountjoy leaving the house last night. She said he had his work boots with him and he didn't come back home. But there's a pair of men's boots in the porch. And when the body was found, he was wearing trainers.'

"Yes, I'd forgotten that. So is she lying—"

"—or did he come home later that night and change his shoes before he was killed?"

CHAPTER 14

"We're not usually this busy on a Monday night," whispered Annie as she squeezed past Charlie and grabbed yet another pint glass.

"Nothing like a juicy bit of gossip to bring in the punters," said Charlie with a grin. "Maybe we could write a book on how to run a successful pub, and recommend a dead body as a good way to build up trade!"

Annie tutted at her and shook her head.

"That's not nice, Charlie. Poor Simon." She paused and looked around at the noisy crowd the other side of the bar. "There doesn't seem to be much mourning going on, does there?"

"Not really, no. But Dave did say he wasn't as popular as maybe he appeared to be."

As they carried on serving, Charlie reflected on silver linings. The pub had been doing okay, especially at the weekends, and the room lettings were slowly rising, but it was clear the reason for the crowded bar this Monday night was word of Simon Mountjoy's death had got around. Plus the fact the police were using one of the upstairs rooms to conduct interviews. Each time the inner door from the bar to the accommodation part of the building squeaked open, there was a slight lull in the conversation and every head craned that way. But so far DCI Harolds and DS Smith hadn't made an appearance. By ten o'clock the crowd of drinkers showed no sign of disappearing.

"I wonder if we should tell them the police had their supper upstairs and then slipped out of the back door an hour ago?" said Annie.

"Not yet." Charlie winked at her. "They've still got time for a couple more drinks. We can tell them when we're ready to close up. Pity the restaurant's closed on Mondays, but we couldn't have managed without Iris in the kitchen. And we've needed the two of us here in the bar."

"That reminds me," said Annie. "The DCI was asking about Iris. I said it was her day off, so she wants to talk to her tomorrow morning, and to both of us as well."

"Actually, I've not seen Iris all day. And I don't think she's in her room yet. She may not know what's been going on."

"We'd better slip a note under her door then, just to warn her. I'll pop up there once we've finished in here."

There was a queue of people clamouring for drinks, and the conversation finished there.

A few minutes later Charlie became aware of shouting in one corner of the bar. It was a woman's voice and from the sound of it, she'd been drinking most of the evening.

"Why are we so worried about how that dreadful man ended up dead? Good riddance, I say."

"Oh dear," said Annie, "Sounds like Pauline's had too much to drink again. You're not still serving her, are you, Charlie?"

"Of course not." Charlie shook her head. "I know better than that after last time. She must have been getting other people to buy drinks for her. But I'm not surprised to hear her views on Simon. She was having a real pop at him on Saturday evening."

Pauline Wilson was the only person the couple had come close to banning from The Falls. In her mid-forties, with shoulder-length auburn hair, she was a quiet, unassuming woman most of the time. She lived alone with her widowed mother and spent all her spare time raising money for an animal charity. Most people spoke highly of Pauline and admired how she looked after her mother, who was starting to slide into dementia.

But Pauline had an alter ego who appeared after she'd had a few drinks. And it was that person shouting the odds at the other end of the bar.

"I'd better go and sort this out." Charlie raised the flap at the end of the bar, but Annie put her hand on her shoulder.

"No, Charlie, let me. Pauline and I've spent quite a bit of time together lately, at our choir rehearsals. Let me talk to her."

Charlie watched Annie cross the room, and put her arm around Pauline's shoulders. She saw her shush the other woman and lead her towards the door. As they reached it, Annie turned and raised her palm with fingers outstretched in the universal sign for five minutes. Pauline Wilson only lived across the road from The Falls, in a two-bedroomed house on the new estate. Charlie assumed Annie was going to see her safely home and then come back. She wasn't sure that was a good idea. After all, there appeared to be a murderer in the village. What if he was out there, looking for his next victim?

"It's alright, Charlie, we'll go and help Annie with Pauline." Charlie turned to find Roger Richardson standing by the bar with three empty glasses in his hand. "Celia and I were just leaving anyway. And you probably won't want Annie out there on her own, now will you?"

Realising her concern must have shown on her face, Charlie gave a relieved smile.

"I'd appreciate that, Roger," she said and winked at him before turning back to serve the next customer. The next time she looked, Annie was back with her behind the bar and the incident was forgotten in the rush for last orders.

"How did you get on with Pauline?" Charlie asked later, as they were closing up for the night. Annie pulled a face and shook her head.

"I feel so sorry for her, Charlie. She's had such a lot to cope with. Imagine one of us trying to look after a parent with dementia on our own. It's no wonder she lets off steam occasionally, when she can get someone to sit with her mum." She went quiet for a few minutes as she loaded glasses into the dishwasher. Then she turned towards Charlie. "I left her sitting on the sofa, half asleep. I offered to help her get to bed, but she said she was going to stay up and watch television for a while. And I could see the Richardsons were in a hurry to get home, so I gave her a hug and left her to it. But as we were walking out of the door, she said 'at least I'll sleep well tonight, knowing that bastard can't do anything more to us. A good day's work, I reckon'."

"Can't do anything more to us? What on earth does she mean?"

"I don't know, Charlie. But maybe there's something about Pauline Wilson we don't know. Something more than just concern over her mother's health, that makes her drink too much."

"We'll have to ask Celia tomorrow," said Charlie. "She seems to know everything that's going on around here. I think another lunch in Cosy Corner's called for, don't you?"

CHAPTER 15: TUESDAY 9TH JULY

When Annie arrived from The Folly just before seven the following morning, she found the kitchen deserted. The kettle was still cold and no-one was there to make a start on frying the eggs and grilling the bacon. She tutted and grabbed the house phone, hitting the keys for Iris's room in the attic. But there was no response. Annie sighed to herself and started getting things ready. She was still sighing and muttering when Charlie arrived half an hour later.

"No Iris?"

"No! And there's no answer from her room either. I wonder where she is?" Annie said. "She's normally so reliable."

"Well, we need her down here. The guests will be wanting their breakfasts soon." Charlie threw down the tea towel she'd been using to wipe plates and picked up the phone. But there was still no answer. "Do you want me to go and bang on her door?" she said. "I know she told us she was a heavy sleeper, but this is ridiculous."

"Yes, please," said Annie. "And while you do, I'll just pop back to The Folly and make sure Suzy's awake."

But when Annie returned ten minutes later, there was a puzzled look on Charlie's face.

"Her room's empty but the door was unlocked! Her bed

doesn't look like it's been slept in, and that old leather sports bag she arrived with has disappeared." She paused and gave a sigh. "Annie, I think she's gone."

"But why would she do that without saying anything to us? Do you think we should call the police?"

"No, let's not do that just yet." Annie knew Charlie's views on the police and authorities in general were slightly more jaundiced than her own. "There might be a perfectly reasonable explanation for all this. Especially if she's taken her stuff with her. You get breakfast started and I'll try and reach Iris on her mobile. I'll do it from the bar, the signal's better in there."

When Annie joined her a few minutes later, Charlie was staring at her phone and shaking her head.

"No answer from her mobile, either. I've tried a couple of times, but it just clicks through to her voice mail."

"How about Facebook? Or Instagram? She's always on there."

"Checked those too. There's nothing been posted since Sunday morning."

"You know, I don't think we've seen her since the lunchtime service finished on Sunday." Annie paused as a sudden shocking thought came to her. "Sunday night! That's when Simon Mountjoy was killed. Maybe she saw something? Maybe she disturbed the killer? Oh, Charlie, do you think she's okay?"

Charlie shook her head.

"I'm sure she's fine, Annie. We don't know where she is, or why she's gone, but she's taken her stuff, remember? Which implies she left of her own free will."

"Yes, I guess you're right. But I'd be happier if we could find her. Just to be sure."

"Look, let's get breakfast over with and then try her phone again. But if we don't get some news about Iris in the next couple of hours, I think you're right. We're going to have to tell the police. She's not going to make her interview with the DCI at this rate."

CHAPTER 16

Charlie glanced up from the catalogue she was flicking through as the door of the bar burst open and Anthony Farsider strode in.

"Are they in? Those detective chappies, are they in?"

"And a good morning to you, too, Anthony." Charlie closed the book with a smile and shook her head. "I'm afraid DCI Harolds and DS Smith are out at the moment. But they said they wouldn't be long. Can I get you a coffee while you're waiting?"

Anthony tutted and looked at his watch.

"No, no, I've just had one." He paused, then apparently remembered his manners. "But, thank you for the offer, Charlie."

For the next fifteen minutes, as Charlie carried on with her preparations for opening time, Farsider marched up and down the bar, periodically checking his watch again and sighing heavily. When the detectives finally walked in, he turned and charged towards them like a turkey cock whose territory was being threatened.

"Now look here, I understand you lot have put a block on all Simon's affairs. You need to get this nonsense sorted out pretty damn quick. There's a major business deal hanging in the balance."

"Two coffees, please, Ms Jones," said the DCI, "and a couple of those chocolate chip cookies." She sidestepped Farsider, undid the buttons on her jacket, slipped it off and hung it over the back of a chair before sitting down, folding her hands in front of her and then, for the first time, looked directly at the man staring indignantly at her.

"And you are...?"

"Farsider, Antony Farsider. Managing director of Farsider-Mountjoy Developments Ltd. This business has all come at a most inconvenient time!"

"By this business, I take it you mean the murder of Mr Simon Mountjoy?"

"Murder? No-one told me it was murder! I suppose that's why they've brought you lot in. I wondered why it wasn't being dealt with locally. How do you know it was murder?"

DS Smith opened his mouth to respond, but at a sharp look from his boss, closed it again. Charlie knew they hadn't released details to the press so far and she guessed they wanted to keep it like that for the moment.

"Let's just say the circumstances were suspicious," Harolds said. Then, pulling her notepad out of her bag, she smiled at Farsider. "As it happens, we were going to come to see you this afternoon, so I guess you've saved us a journey. Do take a seat, Mr Farsider. As soon as we've got our coffee, we'll go somewhere a bit more private."

Their visitor checked his watch again, sighed impatiently and sat down heavily in the chair opposite the DCI.

"Well, alright, but let's make it quick; I'm up to my eyes as it is."

"Here's your coffee," said Charlie. She paused. "And if you want, you can talk to Anthony, I mean Mr Farsider, in here, DCI Harolds. I've got stuff to do in the kitchen and there won't be anyone coming in for another hour or so."

"Thank you, Ms Jones." And as Charlie left through the swing door she heard the DCI continue. "Can you tell us a bit more about this deal you mentioned, Mr Farsider, and why the death of Simon Mountjoy has any effect on it?"

Charlie nipped along the kitchen corridor, turned the corner into the back of the restaurant and silently settled herself at one of the corner tables. From there, she could hear what was going on in the bar, without been seen. Anthony Farsider was talking.

"…set up Farsider-Mountjoy Developments, or FMD as Simon liked to call it, some years ago. Just after he came back to the village in fact. We'd always talked about working together, right back from schooldays. And we kept in touch all the time he was away. Always making plans, he was. He was the ideas man really, the general who gives the orders. I'm the regimental sergeant major who carries them out."

"And yet you introduced yourself as the managing director?"

"That's right, I am. Not that Simon seemed to respect that these days."

"And you're in charge because…?"

"I was the major investor when we started out. Simon didn't have any spare cash when he came home. He was ploughing everything into that house of his. So I put up all the money. Plus I'm the elder by a couple of years. It didn't bother Simon then. He was always happier in the back room. 'I'll leave all the glad-handing and front man stuff to you, Tony' he used to say."

"You said it didn't bother him then. Why 'then', Mr Farsider? What changed?"

"Not 'what changed?' Detective Chief Inspector, but 'who changed?' These past few years, Simon was different. He became much more interested in his public image. He came to all the dinners and other events with me. Everything he used to hate suddenly became important to him. To be honest, I thought he fancied being the next MP for the area, but he just told me I was raving."

"And are you still the major shareholder?"

"I didn't say I was the major shareholder. I said I was the major investor, at one point, the only investor."

"And is that still the situation?"

"No. Over the years, Simon paid back the loan. We set a rule right from the start, that we'd never have a 50:50 split. That can lead to paralysis if the shareholders disagree on a major strategy. We also agreed no-one should own a majority stake in the business. We both own 45%. Another 5% is owned by the workers in the company. We've given them out as Christmas bonuses over the years."

"That makes 95%. Who owns the remainder, Mr Farsider?"

"Oh, we split that between Marion, my wife, and Olga Mountjoy. Look, is this all really necessary? I need to get into Exeter, to see if I can save this deal before it goes 'tits up' if you'll excuse my French, Detective Chief Inspector."

"We're nearly done, Mr Farsider, although we may need to talk to you again later in the week. We need to get as much background information as we can if we're to catch this murderer. So tell me about this deal. What's so important about it?"

"It's a building company from London. They're looking to expand their business down here in the South West and want to merge with a good local company from which to establish a base."

"And they're interested in Farsider-Mountjoy Developments, are they?"

"Oh, they're more than interested, Detective Chief Inspector. They're dead keen. Well we all are, really. They're experts in interiors whereas we specialise in exteriors. They do a lot of new build. We're much more about conversions. It would be the perfect fit. But we're running out of time."

"How so?"

"They've got a shareholders' meeting coming up in September and they want to present this deal for approval. But it's taken longer to reach agreement than it should have, and they've been looking around for other options. They've given us to the end of next week, and then they're going to approach an alternative group instead."

Charlie heard DS Smith give a slight cough. Then the young detective broke in quietly.

"Mr Farsider, why is this deal so important? Is FMD in financial difficulties?"

"Absolutely not!" There was a screech of chair legs on slate. Charlie assumed Anthony Farsider had jumped up. And sure enough, as he continued talking, she realised he must be pacing the room once more. "We're doing very well, young man, very well indeed, despite what people might say. It's just that at our age, one wants to start slowing down, taking things at bit easier, as it were."

"And did Mr Mountjoy feel the same way?"

"Simon was feeling his age too. He was starting to develop other priorities. He was just as happy as me to talk about the deal." There was a pause, then Anthony continued. "I'm sorry, Detective Chief Inspector, I really must go now. My meeting's in less than an hour – and the parking in Exeter at this time of day will be horrendous."

"Thanks for your time, Mr Farsider. We'll be in touch."

There were hurried footsteps in the direction of the front door. Charlie heard the hinges creak.

"Oh, Mr Farsider," called Smith, "for the record, can you tell us where you were between ten pm and four am on Sunday night?"

"In bed, sonny, where else would I be?" was the reply and with a bang of the door, he was gone.

"That didn't sound too convincing," said Smith.

"No, we need to check that one with his wife, I think. And I've a feeling that's not the only time he's lied to us."

"No?"

"No. He sounded very polished when he answered my questions; but did you notice the hesitation when I asked about Simon Mountjoy's views on the deal? I reckon if we dig a bit deeper, we may find there was a hold-up in this deal. I suspect the late unlamented Simon Mountjoy was not as wholeheartedly in favour of selling up as Mr Farsider would have us believe."

As the two detectives headed upstairs to their temporary incident room, Charlie tiptoed back to the kitchen. She'd not been able to watch Anthony Farsider's face, but she also suspected there was more to this deal than he was letting on. She wondered just what the finances of the company looked like.

CHAPTER 17

It was nearly eleven and Charlie was getting the bar ready for the lunchtime service when DS Smith popped his head around the door.

"Ms Jones, can you spare us a few minutes, please?" It was phrased as a question, but Charlie got the distinct impression it was not a request but a summons. She called through to the kitchen and told Annie where she was going. Then with a pointed look at the clock, she followed the young detective upstairs.

"Sit down, Ms Jones," said DCI Harolds. Charlie looked at her watch and parked herself on the edge of the chair. The DCI smiled frostily. "It's alright, I won't keep you very long. I just have a few questions about yesterday's unfortunate events." Charlie thought she made it sound like an argument over a parking space, rather than a brutal murder. But she just nodded, as the DCI continued. "Tell us again about the events leading up to the discovery of the body."

Charlie sighed inwardly and did as she was asked. She knew the police were only doing their duty.

"Now, can you tell us about the previous evening?" was the next question.

"What about it?"

"Well, did you go out into the garden at any time? Did you see anything, hear anything? Did you see Mr Mountjoy by any chance?"

"No, I didn't go into the garden after dark, no. I dropped some empties out the back around eight-thirty and there was no-one to be seen then. The last people left the beer garden around nine. We went back to The Folly around midnight. I walked the babysitter back home."

"Babysitter? No-one mentioned a babysitter before."

"Suzy's only eight, DCI Harolds. Did you think we left her on her own in The Folly every evening? We've got a small group from the village and from Chudleigh who take it in turns to sit with her on the nights we're both working."

"Okay, we'll need the details for whoever was there on Sunday night."

"That would be Melanie from Tulip Cottage, just off the green. Annie sings with her in the choir. She'll have her mobile number. Although I doubt if she can tell you anything. Simon was killed above the weir, wasn't he? In his own grounds?"

"Just tying up loose ends, Ms Jones. And you didn't say whether you saw Mr Mountjoy on Sunday evening or not."

"No, I didn't see Simon on Sunday at all. He was here on Saturday evening for our anniversary party, but he's not, sorry he wasn't, our typical customer. I don't think he'd been in here more than a dozen times in the year we've been open."

The DCI appeared satisfied with Charlie's answers.

"Okay, Ms Jones, so can you tell me about the rest of the staff. Where was Ms McLeod working and who else was on duty?"

Charlie could feel herself bridling and made a conscious effort to keep calm.

"To start with, Ms McLeod is not part of the staff. She's co-owner of this business and my wife. And secondly, if you want to know what she was doing, you need to ask her yourself!"

"Oh, we will, Ms Jones, we will. And the rest of the staff?"

"It was a quiet evening. We only had one other person on. Young Billy from the farm. He does an occasional weekend shift for us. The kitchen's closed on Sunday evenings."

"I believe you have a live-in member of staff?" Harolds consulted her notes, although Charlie had the distinct impression this was for show only. "An Iris Murphy? Where was she that night?"

"Iris? She has Sunday afternoon and all day Monday off. I didn't see her once we'd finished lunch on Sunday."

"And what about since then, Ms Jones? Have you seen Iris Murphy since then? Is she on duty today?"

"Well, she's supposed to be. But, no, we've not seen her today. As I said, yesterday was her day off. She was expected on duty this morning but her room's empty. We're trying to get in touch with her at the moment. Why?"

"Just another loose end, Ms Jones, that's all." The DCI looked at her watch and smiled. "Right, I think we've kept you long enough. But we're going to have to have a quick word with Ms McLeod, I'm afraid."

"She's covering the kitchen in Iris's absence. Do you want me to send her up then?" asked Charlie, but the DCI shook her head.

"No, it's fine, Ms Jones. You go back to the bar. DS Smith will find Ms McLeod and bring her up here." It looked to Charlie as though the DCI didn't want them talking to each other before she had a chance to interview Annie.

The lunchtime trade was quite busy. Charlie assumed it was still a hangover from her early morning discovery the previous day. Annie didn't spend too long in the incident room and was soon back buzzing between the bar and the kitchen with sandwiches and ploughman's lunches. The pair were on their own. The main restaurant didn't open at lunchtime during the week and they rarely had other staff on during the day. So it wasn't until mid-afternoon that they had a chance to swap notes.

"Well, what did the DCI say?" asked Charlie.

"Just the usual questions. Where was I on Sunday evening? Did I go out into the garden? Did I see Simon Mountjoy? When did I last see him?"

"Pretty much the same questions she asked me then."

"I guess so, Charlie, yes. There wasn't much I could tell her. I never went into the garden after Sunday lunchtime, except when we went back to The Folly, and I last saw Simon on Saturday evening." She paused. "But the DCI seemed to be very interested in Iris."

"Yes, she asked me about her too. I told her she was off duty on Sunday and we haven't seen her since."

"You know, Charlie, I'm getting really worried about Iris. Have you tried her phone again?"

Their conversation was interrupted by heavy footsteps on the staircase. Seconds later the DCI and her sergeant came through the door and into the bar.

"Ah, ladies, I'm glad to find you together," said Harolds. "Have you had any luck tracing Iris Murphy yet?" Charlie and Annie both shook their heads. "And neither of you has any idea where she might be?"

"Not a clue," said Charlie. "She's probably gone off with some friends. She'll turn up at some point."

The DCI nodded and the two detectives left.

Charlie and Annie stared at each other.

"You know what this means, don't you?" asked Charlie.

"I need to get on the phone and find a temporary chef to cover tonight's shift?"

"Well yes, that's true. But more importantly, we've told the police we haven't seen Iris since she went off duty on Sunday lunchtime. I suspect she's now officially a missing person."

CHAPTER 18

It was early evening before the two detectives returned to the pub. They took a table in the restaurant and ordered burger and chips twice, although the DCI asked for a salad with hers and gave most of her chips to her sergeant.

When Annie went over to clear their plates, Harolds spoke to her in a low voice.

"You'll be pleased to hear, Ms McLeod, we have someone we urgently want to talk to about the murder of Simon Mountjoy."

"You have? That's quick work. Well done!"

"Aren't you curious to know who it is?"

"Well, yes, of course. But I assumed you wouldn't be able to tell me."

"Oh, it's no secret, Ms McLeod. We've issued a warrant for the arrest of Iris Murphy."

"What? You can't have! That's nonsense. Iris wouldn't hurt a fly! I've never heard her so much as raise her voice to anyone."

"And you've known her how long, Ms McLeod?"

"She came to us the first week we opened after the New Year break, so it must be all of six months – nearly seven now," said Annie, but it sounded weak, even to her. And she suspected the DCI realised that.

"Hardly a lifetime's knowledge is it, Ms McLeod?"

"But why would you think she has anything to do with it?"

"Well, according to Olga Mountjoy, the victim's wife, Iris Murphy was up at Mountjoy Manor on Sunday afternoon. Turned up on the lawn as the couple and their guests were finishing lunch. She demanded to speak to him and he took her into the house. He was gone for so long Mrs Mountjoy went to find him. When she got into the house, there was no sign of them at first, but then she realised they were in his office at the front. She could hear both of them shouting. Then the door flew open and Iris Murphy dashed out and shot straight past her, out through the front door and went running down the drive."

"And did Simon explain to Olga what was going on?"

"No, he didn't, but Mrs Mountjoy says he was distracted for the rest of the afternoon."

"But this doesn't mean Iris had anything to do with the murder, does it?"

"Not on its own, no. But she was shouting threats at Mr Mountjoy as she left the manor. And now she appears to have done a runner. No-one has seen her since before the murder took place. We need to talk to her as soon as possible." The DCI looked sternly at Annie. "You will let us know if either you or Ms Jones hear from your errant chef, won't you, Ms McLeod?"

"Yes, Detective Chief Inspector, of course we will." For a second, Annie was taken right back to her schooldays and being taken to task by one of the nuns for something she was suspected of doing.

"Good." The DCI smiled and picked up the menu. "Right, now I think I might just have room for one of your delicious puddings."

Annie never knew where the information came from. The two detectives had finished their supper and headed back to Exeter. There was no-one from the local police force in the pub. But around ten-thirty, a rumour started circulating. Iris Murphy had been located. She'd been picked up by the police in a café in Birmingham. A team on night duty had stopped off for coffee and recognised her from the picture circulated earlier that day by the Devon and Cornwall constabulary. She was in custody and would be driven back to the South West the following morning.

Annie assumed she'd be taken to the main police station in Exeter, rather than being brought back to Coombesford. But either way, she knew she'd have to try to get permission to see her. She and Charlie hadn't known their talented chef very long. As DCI Harolds had pointed out, seven months was hardly a lifetime. But Annie was usually a good judge of character and she knew without a shadow of a doubt Iris Murphy was no murderer. She'd acted as a babysitter for Suzy on several occasions. There was no way Annie would have trusted her with their daughter if she'd had the slightest concern about her. And she was sure Charlie felt the same way.

No, there had to be some other explanation for why she'd gone to visit Simon Mountjoy. Why they'd argued so fiercely. And why she'd then done a disappearing act straight afterwards, right around the time, or just after, the murder had taken place.

The following morning was supposed to be Annie's time off, her turn for a lie in and the chance to see Suzy off to school while Charlie ran the breakfast shift. Annie volunteered to take the early shift, but told Charlie she'd need some time off later in the morning.

"I'm going to do some digging," she said, "to get to the bottom of all this. There's no way Iris Murphy is a murderer."

CHAPTER 19: WEDNESDAY 10TH JULY

DCI Harolds and DS Smith arrived at just after seven the next morning, and for the second day running, grabbed a table for breakfast. Harolds was humming to herself as she poured milk on her cornflakes, and even Smith managed a bit of a smile when Annie served him his full English.

"Might as well make the most of it," he said, as he ladled tomato sauce over everything. "The wife won't normally let me have this."

Annie looked up in surprise.

"You're leaving?"

The DCI nodded.

"Yes, we're finished here for the moment. We've got a couple more interviews this morning and that's the lot for now. We'll be packing up the incident room as soon as we've finished; I hope to be out of here by mid-afternoon. If you could sort out our bill, Ms McLeod, that would be very helpful."

"And Iris?"

"Yes, Ms McLeod, we've got her. The West Midlands guys picked her up last night and are driving her down here as we speak. In a couple of hours, she'll be safely in custody in Exeter. You'll have us out of your hair this afternoon, and once the forensics people have confirmed they have everything from the crime scene, you can have your garden back as well."

"And you really think…"

"Oh, we certainly do, Ms McLeod. It's all circumstantial at the moment, but we're pretty confident of getting a confession out of her. She seemed quite resigned, according to the custody sergeant who booked her into Colmore Row police station last night." Harolds picked up the teapot, shook it and put it down again. "I think we'll have a drop more water in here, if that's okay, Ms McLeod." And with a satisfied smile, she applied herself to her bowl of cereal.

As Annie headed for the kitchen with the empty teapot, her mind was buzzing.

When Charlie returned from her morning walk around the village, Annie was pacing up and down in the bar, chewing her thumbnail.

"They won't let me see her!" she burst out as soon as her wife walked through the door. "Iris is all alone in that dreadful place and they won't let me see her."

"Annie, you make it sound like something out of the Victorian era. I'm sure it's not that bad these days."

"But she's all alone, Charlie! She's got no relatives here in Devon. In fact, I'm not sure she's got any family at all. She's never mentioned anyone. How's she going to cope? Just imagine if it was our Suzy. You'd hope someone would want to visit her and support her, wouldn't you?"

"Yes, of course I would, and we'll give her all the support we can." Charlie paused. "But the police seem to think they have a good case, Annie. Why are you so sure she's innocent?"

"The police! Huh! They're just looking for the easy way out. A murder in a rural area. An easy suspect. Case closed!"

"Hey, that's usually my line," said Charlie. "You're not usually the cynical one. What's got into you?"

"I don't know, Charlie," Annie said with a sigh. "Call it intuition, call it gut feeling. But I just don't think she did it.

And until she looks me in the eye and tells me yes or no, I'd rather think better of her, than worse."

"So when will you be able to see her? Did they say?"

"Apparently, she's being interviewed later today. And it all depends on whether they've got enough to charge her or not."

"Well, okay; let's wait and see what happens." Charlie looked around the bar and the restaurant, where there were dirty dishes still on the tables from breakfast. "Right, Annie, let's get this place cleared up. We've still got a pub to run. And we're missing our chef, don't forget. We managed okay last night, but if they do charge her, we may be without Iris for a good while. If she wants to come back at all, that is. I'd better get on to the agency and see if they can find a temp at short notice."

Annie nodded and walked across to the restaurant to start clearing the tables. Then she turned back to Charlie.

"We're going to have to do it ourselves, aren't we?"

"Do what, Annie?"

"Find out what really happened to Simon Mountjoy. If Iris didn't do it – and I'm sure she didn't – then someone else did. Quite possibly someone from this village. Someone we know."

"Yes, I guess you're right," said Charlie reluctantly.

"We need to investigate! Just like you and Suzanne did when you were working together. We'll start by asking a few questions, see where that leads us. We're right in the middle of everything here. All sorts of things get said in the bar, especially after a few drinks. It's the best possible place to be."

"Apart from Cosy Corner, of course," said Charlie slowly. Annie stopped what she was doing and nodded excitedly.

"You're right! Between us and Cosy Corner, we must see most of the villagers at least once a week."

"Plus there's the church and the school."

"Yes, those too, Charlie. But let's start with what we've

72

got. We'll cover here. But when it comes to Cosy Corner…should we talk to Richard or Celia, do you think? Tell them our thoughts?"

Charlie shook her head.

"Can't do that, not yet. Remember how Richard behaved when he heard Simon was dead? He definitely didn't like the man at all. So I'm afraid Richard's on the suspects list at the moment. Which means Celia is too." She paused and then grinned. "No, I've a better idea. Remember Celia was talking about needing some more help in the café? I think it's time to deploy our secret weapon, don't you?"

Annie laughed and nodded her head.

"Oh yes, I think that's a great idea. And that'll certainly liven things up a bit."

Charlie turned back to the tables.

"Right. I'll get this lot into the kitchen and then get on the phone. It's time I renewed an old acquaintance."

CHAPTER 20

Charlie was tidying up in the bar after the lunchtime session when the outside door swung open.

"I'm afraid you're too late," she called, not looking up, "we've just closed."

"It's alright, Ms Jones, we're not here for a drink," was the unexpected reply. "We've just come to leave someone with you."

Charlie spun round as DCI Harolds walked across to the bar, followed by DS Smith and Iris Murphy. Charlie gasped. When she and Annie had first met Iris, they'd taken her for someone in her mid-twenties and had been amazed to find she was actually ten years older than that. Usually so careful about her appearance, today she was wearing no makeup, her clothes looked crumpled and slept in, she had bags under her eyes, and her wavy chestnut brown hair could definitely do with a wash. She stood with her head down, as though waiting to be told what to do.

"We've released Ms Murphy without charge for the time being," Harolds continued. "But we're not finished with her yet. We expect to have more questions for her later in the week. But in the meantime, we've asked her to stay in the village and not do another disappearing act. And she's promised she'll do that."

As the detectives headed upstairs to their temporary base, Charlie sat at one of the tables and gestured to Iris to join her. Once seated, the other woman looked up and glared at her.

"I suppose you're going to have a go at me about doing a disappearing act, too?" she said. She stuck a finger to her lips and began nibbling on a nail that was already chewed to the quick. Charlie shook her head and reached across the table to gently pull her hand away from her mouth.

"No, of course I'm not going to have a go at you," she said. "I'm here to help. Annie and I were really worried about you. Annie's going to be delighted to see you back."

"I'm fine, Charlie. It's all a mistake." The girl shrugged and stared at Charlie with what would have been a much more hostile look, if it hadn't been accompanied by a slight wobble of her chin and hazel eyes that shone unnaturally brightly.

Well, you don't look fine, sweetheart, thought Charlie. *You look like someone who needs some help.* She smiled at her.

"Of course it's a mistake. We know you didn't kill Simon Mountjoy. And we're going to keep telling the police that until they believe us."

The tears in Iris's eyes spilled over onto her cheeks and she slumped down in her seat, like a balloon someone had popped. Charlie jumped up and wrapped her arms around the other woman and made soothing noises as she sobbed. After a few minutes, Iris pulled away from her, sat up and blew her nose, before giving Charlie a watery smile.

"Sorry, Charlie, I've been so scared. It's wonderful to have someone who believes in me."

"Of course it is," said Charlie, realising a business-like approach was probably best if she didn't want Iris to start crying again. "Right, now the question is, how can we persuade the police they've got it wrong?"

Iris shrugged her shoulders but said nothing. Charlie had another try.

"Why don't you tell me what happened on Sunday? The

police seem to think you visited Mountjoy Manor in the afternoon before you disappeared. Is that true?"

"Well, I went for a walk up that way, if that's what you mean."

"Olga told the police you burst in on their lunch party, mouthing off at Simon, and he took you into his office. Apparently you were in there for some time and there was shouting, some sort of argument."

"Oh, I didn't realise you knew that." Iris sighed. "Yes, I did go to see Simon and no," she held up a hand as Charlie opened her mouth to ask another question, "I can't tell you why. But I can promise you I never saw him again after I left the house that afternoon."

"Okay, Iris. I don't understand why you can't tell me more, but let's leave that for now. What happened after that?"

"I decided I was going to have to leave. I went back to The Falls, packed my bag and left. I hitched a lift to Exeter and then took a bus to Bristol. The following day I took another one to Birmingham. I've got some old friends in the catering trade there and I thought I'd be able to get a job with one of them while I decided what I wanted to do next."

"But you were recognised and that's how they picked you up?"

"That's right. Apparently they knew I was in the area. I used my credit card to buy my bus ticket and then to pay for my hotel. Why wouldn't I? I didn't know Simon was dead. I realised at the last minute they were looking for me, but I'd left it too late to get away."

"What time did you leave Coombesford on Sunday?" Charlie asked. She didn't understand why Iris wouldn't be completely open with her. Annie adamantly refused to believe their chef was a killer; but if she wasn't prepared to tell them the full story, it was going to be difficult to prove it to the police – or even to herself, Charlie admitted.

"It was about four-thirty."

"And what about the person that you hitched a lift with?

Can't they provide you with an alibi?"

Iris pursed her lips and shook her head slowly.

"The police asked me that. I'm sorry, Charlie, I can't remember anything about them. I was pretty upset." Then she held up a finger. "Although, I remember he was really nice, easy to talk to. And he offered to buy me a coffee when we got to Exeter."

"I don't suppose you got a name, did you?"

"No."

"And the car? Do you remember anything about that?"

"I think it was purple. Or maybe red. Perhaps it was orange." She shook her head and sighed. "I wasn't really paying attention."

"Not to worry," said Charlie, "it's a start. But if you remember anything else, write it down." She looked at her watch. "Right, I've got to pop into Exeter to meet someone, so I'll have to leave you on your own for a while. Annie's shopping in Newton Abbot but she'll be back very soon. Why don't you go and have a shower and a rest. We can manage without you in the kitchen tonight." She rested her hand on Iris's shoulder for a moment. "Just hang on in there, okay? We'll get this sorted. Oh, and Iris," she said, as she picked up her car keys from behind the bar and headed for the door, "no more running, right? It won't do your case any good if you do another disappearing act."

CHAPTER 21

Charlie was sitting in the coffee bar at Exeter Station, nursing a long-cooled mug of instant coffee and wondering if she was wasting her time, when she heard a commotion from the counter.

"I don't care how long it is since you've had anything to drink; you're not coming in here like that!" The large woman behind the counter folded her arms under her pendulous breasts, and glared at the pathetic character standing in front of her. Wearing a greasy grey-green mac that trailed to the floor and a bright purple bobble hat over long white locks, the man was holding out his filthy hands as though they were Oliver Twist's bowl. But he obviously wasn't going to get more, or indeed anything at all, from this harridan.

Charlie sighed, swallowed the rest of her coffee and got to her feet. She hated to see mistreatment, especially of underdogs.

"What does he want?" she asked.

"Can of Coke and a sandwich. But look at the state of him! And I doubt if he's got any money! I can't have him in here. It'll upset the rest of my customers!"

Only if they're as heartless as you, thought Charlie. But she just smiled sweetly at the other woman and held out a tenner.

"Here, let me." And as the woman opened her mouth to argue, she continued, "It's alright. I'll take him outside." She turned to the silent figure next to her and pushed the can and sandwich pack into his arms. "Come on, let's go out in the sunshine. You can eat this out there."

She led the way to a bench on the forecourt and seated herself at one end – as far away as she could from the coat that trailed across the seat, as her companion threw himself down and ripped open the packet. She watched as he swallowed the two cheese salad sandwiches in rapid succession and took a long swig from the can, before belching loudly and sitting back with a sigh.

"Hello, Charlie!"

"Hello, Rohan." She shook her head. "Tell me, you idiot, which part of arriving discreetly did you not understand?"

Rohan Banerjee had been a keen actor throughout his schooldays and the leading light of the Amateur Dramatic Society during his three years at Bath Spa University. However, his attempts to get a place at a number of provincial theatres had met with failure and after two years, his father withdrew his generous allowance and insisted on his youngest son getting a job. Rohan finally accepted he was never going to be the next Irrfan Khan, and the police force was the only other profession that really attracted him.

In the right place at the right time, he'd been seconded to an important sting operation, made a name for himself as an undercover agent, and from then on he was often in demand. His last expedition into the criminal underworld had been working behind the bar in a large pub/restaurant in Newcastle which had developed a bit of a reputation as a drug exchange. He'd done a three-month stint, in the course of which he'd identified several major figures in the county lines drugs scene while still managing to maintain his cover. When he left the week after the dealers were taken into custody, the regulars, including several associates of the villains, had thrown a going away party for him, which had gone on for thirty-six hours and resulted in several drunk driving charges and one drunk and disorderly.

Then, during the trial, the combination of clever questioning by the defence barrister and a careless response by a nervous young PC giving evidence for the first time, meant Rohan's cover was blown. He returned to normal duties, but quickly found the life of a copper dull after undercover work. Resigning from the Force, he'd moved to London, and found work with a small team of private detectives. Which is where Charlie had first met him. They'd worked together on a couple of local projects in the early 2000s and had kept in touch ever since. And he'd jumped at the chance of a trip to the South West when she'd called him that morning.

"Hiding in plain sight, Charlie," he said now with a grin. "It's always the best policy."

"Fair enough." Charlie stood up. "But you are NOT getting in my car looking like that. Ditch the coat and hat, and definitely ditch that wig. And go and have a wash in the station restrooms." She looked at her watch. "But please get a move on. The pub opens in an hour and Annie's all on her own back there."

Once they'd closed up for the night, Charlie and Annie filled their guest in on the events of the past few days. Together they concocted a suitable CV which they popped in an envelope with a short covering letter.

Dear Mrs Richardson

I wish to apply for the position of part-time waiter at Cosy Corner, as advertised in last week's Mid-Devon Advertiser. My experience for the job is shown on the attached CV and I look forward to meeting you and discussing the position further.

Yours sincerely
Rohan Banerjee

While they were waiting for Rohan to stroll across the green and deliver the letter to the café, Charlie and Annie chatted about how they could keep in touch with him without it being too obvious.

"Of course, with his experience from Newcastle, Rohan could be very useful here in the evenings, couldn't he?" said Annie.

"Good point. How about if we ask him to do some evening shifts?"

"And that would leave me free to cover for Iris in the kitchen."

"She's not up to coming back to work then?" asked Charlie.

Annie pulled a face.

"She'll get there, Charlie, but I don't think we should push her too hard. Besides, Suzy was delighted to hear she was getting her heroine as a babysitter tonight. Let's give it a few days and see how it goes."

Of course, thought Charlie, *if the police find more evidence against her, she might not be here at all.* But she knew that was a thought she needed to keep to herself for the time being.

CHAPTER 22: THURSDAY 11TH JULY

When Roger Richardson joined his wife in the café the following morning, she was sitting at one of the tables staring out of the window, a piece of paper clutched in her hand and several other sheets spread out in front of her.

"The post's early today, isn't it?" he asked.

"What?" Celia seemed miles away and jumped at the sound of his voice. "Oh, no, this was delivered by hand." She pushed the sheets across towards him. "It's someone answering my advert in the MDA. Sounds quite promising too. You have a look while I get you a coffee."

As Roger picked up the CV and covering letter, he wondered what had happened to the other paper, the one in Celia's hand. He could have sworn that was cream. But everything in front of him was standard white office paper. Maybe he'd been mistaken.

"What do you think?" Celia asked, handing him his mug. "I quite like the sound of him."

"Yes, me too. There's a mobile number here. Give him a ring and get him to come in for a chat. If he's as good as he sounds on paper, he can start straight away."

"Well, I think we'll give him a chance to wake up first," said Celia with a laugh, pointing to the clock. "Not everyone starts their day before eight, now do they?" She took another sip of coffee and went back to staring out of the window.

"True." He paused. "Is everything alright, love? You seem a bit distracted this morning."

"I'm fine. Just planning the baking for the rest of the week. Now, why don't you go and see if any of the hoppers need refilling before opening time?"

Roger did as she suggested. But when he came out of the stockroom, Celia was staring at that bit of paper once more. Maybe it was just a shopping list, he thought. But somehow he didn't quite believe it.

Celia made a phone call just after nine. At ten o'clock precisely, a neat, slim man in his mid-thirties came through the door.

"Mrs Richardson," Roger heard him say, "how do you do? I'm Rohan Banerjee. I'm here about the job?"

There was much laughter from the table where the two sat and talked. Roger was not at all surprised when Celia called him over during a lull in customers.

"Roger, meet Rohan." The man stood and held out his hand to Roger, bowing respectfully. "He's going to be working here lunchtimes and Saturdays. And he's starting straight away."

"Well, that's grand, Celia. Welcome to Coombesford, Rohan. What brings you to this part of the country?"

"I'm an old friend of Charlie Jones, Mr Richardson. I'm down here for the summer helping her and Annie out in the evenings, but my days are going to be free and when I saw your advert, I thought I'd give it a shot. And Mrs Richardson is kind enough to have taken me on."

"Now, enough of that Mr and Mrs nonsense," said Celia. "We don't stand on ceremony here in Coombesford. It's Celia and Roger from now on." She stood up and pointed her head towards the kitchen. "Come on, I'll show you the ropes. I don't suppose you have any baking experience, do you?"

As Roger returned to his counter, he reflected on the

change in Celia since this morning. She was smiling much more. But later, he caught her staring at that bit of paper for ages. What on earth was going on?

CHAPTER 23

By eight o'clock that evening, the bar of The Falls was heaving once more. Charlie wondered if it was tempting fate to hope they'd have more incidents like this once summer gave way to autumn, to keep everyone coming out and chasing the gossip. Not more murders of course. That was just too ghoulish for words. But maybe a juicy scandal or two. Just until the Christmas party season kicked in.

"Phew, this is a bit of a crush, isn't it?" said Annie as she sped past holding a tray of desserts for a table of early diners in the restaurant. "I'm glad we managed to persuade Rohan to help us out. How's he doing?"

"He's doing just fine," said Charlie. They both glanced across at their new temporary barman who'd made quick work of learning the till system and was now serving a large party at one end of the bar while maintaining a conversation with a young couple ensconced at the other end. "I think we may have found a treasure there."

"At some point, we're going to have to ask him just how long he's willing to stay. Although, I got the impression business isn't exactly booming in London at the moment."

"Yes, I guessed that, when he was able to come down here at a moment's notice. But let's not get ahead of ourselves. I'm just delighted to have more help. And hopefully, Iris will feel up to coming back to work in the next day or so."

The two spent the next couple of hours rushing around and didn't have time to stop and chat at all. At one point, Charlie slipped through the door behind the bar into the passageway, just to get her breath back. She surveyed the crowd through the small leaded glass window. Roger and Celia Richardson were sitting in one corner, chatting with Pauline Wilson. The three had shared a light supper and a bottle of non-alcoholic wine. The couple from Cosy Corner appeared to have taken on the role of keeping Pauline more or less sober. No doubt they didn't want a repeat of Monday night's performance when they'd had to help carry her home.

Anthony Farsider had called in around nine to book a table for the weekend. He seemed much more relaxed than during his meeting with DCI Harolds and DS Smith. He'd spotted a neighbour of his at the bar, and as Charlie watched through her window, he was still there with a half-full pint glass in front of him.

Just before ten-thirty, Charlie was surprised to see Hilda Reynolds push her way through the door and pause uncertainly on the threshold. She wasn't a regular customer of theirs. In fact Charlie wasn't sure she'd ever served her before, apart from at the anniversary party. Was that really less than a week ago? So much had happened since. Now, Charlie watched as the other woman approached the bar and stood looking around vaguely, as though searching for someone.

"Ms Reynolds, good evening. What can I get you?" she asked in her best mine-host voice. The woman gave a start and looked directly at her for the first time.

"Oh, no, sorry, I'm not here for a drink."

"Supper then? Did you want a table? The kitchen's about to close but…"

But the other woman shook her head impatiently and held up a hand to cut Charlie off.

"No, I don't want anything to eat, or to drink, thank you." She paused, shook her head. "I er, I just…" Her voice trailed off. Then she straightened her back and said firmly, "I'd like a quick word with you, if possible."

Charlie looked around and pulled a face.

"Well, it's not really a good time," she said, but seeing Hilda's frown begin to turn into something more desperate, she hurriedly changed her mind and called out across the bar, "Rohan, can you manage on your own for a minute or two?"

On getting a thumbs up from her new barman, she lifted the end of the counter and cocked her head to invite the other woman through. She pushed open the back door and waited until the two of them were out in the passageway at the bottom of the stairs. "Okay, it's a bit quieter out here. What can I do for you, Ms Reynolds?"

"Ms Jones, am I right in thinking Iris Murphy is back here at The Falls?"

"Yes, you are. Although she's not on duty at the moment. We've given her a couple of nights off."

"And has she said anything about what happened at the weekend and why the police are interested in her?"

"Oh, I don't think I can answer that. It's up to Iris…"

"Presumably you know about the argument at Mountjoy Manor on Sunday afternoon?"

"Well, yes, the police mentioned that when they first started looking for Iris."

"Did they happen to mention I was there too?"

"No, they didn't." Charlie paused. "But I have to tell you, Annie doesn't believe Iris is guilty."

For the first time since she arrived, the other woman seemed to relax and she smiled. "Oh neither do I, Ms Jones, neither do I." She turned back to the door. "Right, I've kept you from your duties long enough. I must be going. But please give Iris my best wishes."

As if summoned up by the sound of her name, Iris chose that moment to appear at the top of the stairway. When she saw who Charlie was talking to, she shook her head violently and put her finger to her lips. Charlie shrugged and followed her visitor through the door. Glancing back, she saw Iris peering through the window but making no move to follow them.

Back in the bar, the Richardsons and Pauline Wilson were about to leave. Pauline was walking much straighter than she had last time she'd been in, but her voice was just as loud.

"Oh, no, I don't believe Iris Murphy killed Simon Mountjoy," Charlie heard her say. "In fact, I know she didn't. And I'm going to see that Detective Chief Inspector tomorrow morning to tell her exactly what I do know."

The three left the bar, closely followed by Hilda Reynolds. The crowd had thinned out while the two women had been talking out in the passageway. Now, looking around, Charlie saw there was just a handful of customers left, including Anthony Farsider. His neighbour had gone and he was just about to finish his pint. But as Charlie looked at him, his arm was frozen in mid-air, and he was staring transfixed at the closing front door.

CHAPTER 24

Later as they cashed up and watched Rohan clearing up the empty glasses, Annie asked Charlie what Hilda Reynolds had wanted.

"It was quite strange, really," she said. "She wanted to know what Iris had said about the weekend. And she asked me to pass on her good wishes."

"So she obviously doesn't believe Iris killed Simon Mountjoy?"

"Absolutely not. She's convinced of her innocence."

"Well, that's good, isn't it?"

"Yes, I guess so. But the question is, why does she think that? Is it because she knows what really happened? And how does she know Iris, for that matter?"

"That's three questions, Charlie," said Annie with a laugh.

"Okay, but we need to have another look at those suspects of ours. And maybe we need to add Ms Hilda Reynolds to the list."

By the time all the clearing up was finished, it was just after midnight.

"Oh dear," said Annie, glancing up at the big backwards clock on the wall behind the bar. "I'm on the early shift tomorrow morning, or should I say this morning, and I haven't finished laying out the tables yet."

Charlie was standing at the door to the beer garden, gazing out over the darkened valley. The sky was clear and the only lights to be seen were the dazzling array of constellations above their heads. It was cooler and less airless than during the day, but still warm enough for short sleeves.

"It's beautiful out here, Annie," she said, turning back towards the bar. "Let's go and sit outside for a few moments. Rohan wants to share his early findings with us. Let's listen to what he has to say and then we'll finish getting ready for tomorrow. I'm not really sleepy yet, are you?"

"Well no, I suppose not." Annie sighed. "There's been so much going on, my brain's finding it hard to switch off."

"Precisely. Do you want something to drink? It's a bit late for coffee. How about a hot chocolate?"

"Oh, that sounds perfect, Charlie. And do we have any of those…"

"…tiny marshmallows? Yes, of course we do. Rohan, do you want one, too?"

Within a few minutes, the trio were seated together at one of the roughened wooden tables, cupping their hands around matching mugs foaming with hot chocolate and slowly melting marshmallows. Charlie gave a deep sigh of satisfaction.

"I don't care what time of year it is. You can't beat a late night hot chocolate." Then she sat up, put her mug on the table and turned to face the others. "Right, Rohan, you go first. What have you picked up so far?"

"Well, I think it's fair to say there was no love lost between this Simon Mountjoy and some of the other villagers."

"Yes, despite appearances when he was here on Saturday evening," said Annie, "we're beginning to realise he wasn't running for Mr Popularity."

"But that's about the only thing he wasn't running for, according to the gossip – and boy, can some of these folks gossip. For instance, he was campaigning to become mayor next year, did you know that?"

"I'm not even sure we knew Coombesford had a mayor," said Annie. "It's a bit small for that, isn't it?"

"Apparently, they used to just be called Chairman of the Council. But someone decided being called mayor gives them more credibility with the other towns and villages."

"Makes sense, I guess."

"So your Mr Mountjoy gets himself a place on the Parish Council a few years back, see, and then he starts taking part in all sorts of charity events, representing the council or as a personal benefactor. It didn't much matter to him, I understand. And he starts telling people what a good mayor he'd make."

"But if he's so unpopular, how come he was elected to the Parish Council in the first place?"

"Easy really. Not enough candidates! There are seven places on the Coombesford Parish Council, see, and the amount of people willing to stand is always so low, they haven't had an election for about twelve years. Anyone willing to put their name forward, with a couple of nomination signatures, automatically gets elected, if the total number of candidates is below seven."

"And he managed to get enough signatures, did he?"

"Yep, no problem at all. There's a little group of followers that are willing to support him in anything he wants to do. Or should I say, wanted to do."

"Well, they'll have to look for another mayoral candidate now, won't they?"

"Oh, there's one of those already in place. He's been around all along. A nasty piece of work by all accounts, local farmer, bit of a bully, but with a lot of influence in the area. Goes by the name of Tommy Steele—yes, really! At one time, Simon Mountjoy was a great friend of his and was supporting him for mayor, but for some reason, he changed his mind and announced he was going to run himself."

"So if those two had gone head to head, who was the

smart money on?"

"Too close to call, according to the locals. But the bully boy farmer was in for a coffee this afternoon, and I tell you, he had a smile from ear to ear."

CHAPTER 25

"Now, that is interesting," said Charlie. "We've not come across him at all. What else did you find out, Rohan?"

"There's been a bit of a spat between Roger Richardson and the guy running the shop on the new estate. The wags are calling it the Grocery Wars. Hard to believe for such a small village, but it's got two grocery stores. Cosy Corner's been around for years. Roger and Celia are the third generation to run it. Business is a bit tight, especially with the growth of online shopping but they're surviving. Although I suspect that's mainly down to Celia's wonderful cakes in the café."

"So what's the problem?"

"Well Farsider-Mountjoy Developments Ltd owns some of the properties on the new estate and they let one of them to another grocer. And if that wasn't bad enough, rumour has it he was being financed by Simon Mountjoy."

"Ouch."

"Yes; this all happened eighteen months ago, so before you guys arrived. There were letters in the paper, comments at Parish Council meetings, and even a stand-up row in the Co-op in Chudleigh that almost turned into fisticuffs. Apparently, Roger threatened to 'sort Simon Mountjoy out once and for all'. In front of witnesses."

"Did he now? That might explain his reaction to Simon's death."

"I suppose someone's already told you about the scandal over the charity event, haven't they?"

Charlie looked at Annie, then they both shook their heads.

"Er, no."

"Well, it was a couple of years back. Some woman started a campaign to raise money for an animal charity. Something to do with fostering stray kittens, I think."

"This wouldn't be Pauline Wilson, by any chance, would it?" asked Charlie.

"That's the name, yes."

"She was in here tonight, Rohan. She was the one insisting Iris is innocent," said Annie.

"Oh, her," said Rohan. "I had a chat to her when they first arrived. Seemed harmless enough." He took a gulp of his drink and went on. "Well apparently Mountjoy hears about it and goes to the set-up meeting, makes a big donation, with the press there and all. Everyone's so pleased with him, Pauline invites him to be a sponsor for the campaign, which he accepts 'reluctantly'." Rohan used his fingers to make speech marks around this last word. "So he comes up with all sorts of ideas, gets them to organise lots of events, promises to bring in all his mates from the Tories and the golf club. That sort of thing. Then he loses interest after about six months and moves on to the next big thing. The high visibility event is a real washout and all the money disappears. The charity fades away. But someone told me this afternoon Pauline blames Mountjoy for the whole thing. She was overheard in a pub in Newton Abbot at the time, saying what she's not going to do to Mr Simon High-and-Mighty Mountjoy is nobody's business." Rohan leaned back and tucked his hands behind his head. "That's about it for now. But I'm sure there'll be more in the next few days."

"That's brilliant, Rohan," said Charlie. "Right, time for a quick recap, I think." She held up her hand and started ticking off on her fingers as she continued to talk. "When we were in Cosy Corner on Monday, Roger Richardson made no secret of the fact he hated Simon Mountjoy and wasn't sorry to hear he was dead. And Rohan has provided the background to that. So he's on our suspect list. And by association, so is Celia, I'm afraid. I reckon there's nothing that woman wouldn't do for her husband."

"Oh, surely not? She's always been so kind to us every time we've been in there," said Annie before shrugging and nodding. "You're right of course, we can't rule someone out just because they seem nice." She paused then added, "I'm afraid Pauline Wilson has also been very public about her problem with our victim."

"In fact, we now know she's also threatened him in front of witnesses. So yes, she goes on the list."

"And what about this Tommy Steele character?" asked Rohan.

"No, I don't see it, myself," said Annie. The others looked at her in surprise. She shook her head. "Some of the regulars were talking about him the other day. He's certainly not the most popular guy in the village, but they were saying how much they admired him. He's a widower with a grown up daughter at home. She suffers from some sort of agoraphobia, never leaves the farm. Apparently he's devoted to her. Can't see him doing anything to risk leaving her alone, can you?"

"Fair point," said Charlie. "And, let's face it, the mayor's chain hardly seems like a motive for murder, does it? We'll give him the benefit of the doubt for the moment. Anyone else?"

"What about Hilda Reynolds?" asked Annie. Charlie ticked off another finger.

"Yes. After that strange conversation we had this evening, there's definitely something going on there, although I can't work out what it is." She paused and then clicked her fingers. "And then there's that business partner of his, Anthony Farsider."

"You think it might have been him?" asked Rohan.

"It's a possibility. I just happened to be in the restaurant when he was here with the detectives on Tuesday morning. He was shouting the odds about some deal or other that was going pear-shaped. I got the impression he was infuriated, rather than upset, to hear of Simon's demise."

They all sat in silence for a moment, then Annie stirred and shook her head.

"It's all a bit circumstantial, isn't it?

Charlie nodded.

"Yes, I'm afraid you're right. There's nothing here to convince the police they should look any further than Iris Murphy."

"Of course, statistically," said Rohan, "most murders are committed by those closest to the victim. Have we got the grieving widow on the list, Charlie?"

"We don't know much about her, to be honest. But we certainly need to hear what Mrs Olga Mountjoy has to say for herself. I'll see if I can come up with an excuse to go and see her."

But Annie shook her head and put her hand on Charlie's shoulder.

"No, let me do that one. She was in the restaurant with that trainer of hers tonight, and we got chatting. I asked a couple of questions about Mountjoy Manor and told her I used to be an estate agent. She told me to pop over one day; said she'd give me a tour of the place and I could tell her whether I thought there was a chance of a quick sale and how much she'd make. I'll take her up on her offer and see what I can find out." She drained her cup and stood up, holding out her hand to pull Charlie to her feet. "And now, I'm definitely going to bed. Otherwise our guests will be getting their own breakfasts in the morning. Rohan, can we leave you to lock up? I'll finish laying the tables tomorrow."

CHAPTER 26: FRIDAY 12TH JULY

At eight-fifty the following morning, Annie had just finished serving breakfast and Charlie was sitting at one of the tables in the bar, writing out a list for the trip she was due to make to the wholesalers. There were sirens in the distance, but no-one took any notice. Accidents were a common occurrence on the nearby A38, especially during rush hour. But as the sound got closer, Charlie lifted her head and looked towards the door.

"That sounds like it's coming up the lane," she said.

As the two women stared through the window, there was a shout from the entrance to the new estate, just across the road from the pub. Roger Richardson was standing in the middle of the road, waving his arms urgently in the air. At that moment, the sirens became even louder as a police car shot out of the lane, drove around the green and skidded to a halt next to the gesticulating man. It was closely followed by an ambulance, which drove around the police car and turned right into the estate.

"That doesn't look good," said Charlie. "I'll go and see what's happening."

By the time Annie had chivvied Suzy up from the breakfast table, hugged her, popped her lunch box in her bag and pushed her towards the front door, Charlie was back.

"Can't see what's happening," she said, "and I didn't want to get in the way, but it looks like they've all gone into Pauline's house."

"Oh dear," said Annie. "I do hope it's nothing serious. But no doubt we'll hear about it in good time. Right, Suzy, off you go. The bell's due to ring any minute now."

They watched their daughter cross to the middle of the green and over the other side of the road, entering the school gate with a quick backward wave.

"She's growing up fast," said Charlie. "She'll be off to secondary school before we know it."

"Yes," said Annie with a sniff, "and she'll have to learn to get ready a bit quicker then. Look, there's no-one else in the playground. She lives the closest and she's always the last one to arrive!" Shaking her head, she turned back to the restaurant to clear the tables while Charlie got back to her shopping list.

It was just before eleven thirty and the couple were preparing for the lunchtime trade when the outer door opened and Roger Richardson strode in.

"Hello, Roger," said Annie, "we don't normally see you in here during the day. Coffee?"

"No thanks, Annie," he said. "I just popped over during a quiet moment in the café." They both gazed at him expectantly. "I saw you come out during all the commotion earlier, Charlie. I'm afraid there's been another incident. Pauline's been attacked."

"That's terrible," said Charlie. "What happened?"

"When her mother came down this morning, she found Pauline on the floor, unconscious and covered in blood. The medics think she'd been there for several hours. Elsie tried to phone for an ambulance, but got confused and hit the speed dial button instead, so the call came through to us at the café. I called the emergency services and then dashed over there."

"Is she going to be okay?" asked Annie.

"Too soon to tell, Annie. Too soon to tell."

"Burglary, was it?" This from Charlie.

"I think the police are keeping an open mind. Elsie didn't think anything was missing. But I'm not sure the poor woman was in any state to judge that, even without the shock she's had this morning. Mind you, there was no sign of forced entry."

"So she must have known her attacker?" asked Annie.

Roger shrugged.

"Certainly a possibility, yes."

"Well, at least we know one thing," said Annie. "Iris Murphy didn't do this. She was up in her room all night. The downstairs alarm was on and she couldn't have got out without setting it off. So that suggests she's completely innocent, doesn't it?"

"That's bit of a leap, Annie," said Charlie with a chuckle. "Besides, the two crimes might be totally unrelated."

"Right," said Roger, "I must be getting back. Celia and your friend Rohan are covering for me but the café starts to get busy right around now."

"Well," said Annie, as the door swung closed behind him, "what do you think of that? Two serious crimes in a small village in less than a week. Do you really think it's a coincidence, Charlie?"

"Absolutely not! I don't believe in coincidences, remember? The two incidents have to be linked."

"Which proves what I said about Iris was true, doesn't it?"

"Unless of course she had an accomplice?"

Annie spun round and stared at her wife.

"What're you saying, Charlie? Iris is innocent, remember? So she can't possibly have an accomplice, now can she?"

"No, I guess you're right. Sorry, wasn't thinking straight." Charlie decided this wasn't the time to point out they really should have Iris on their list of suspects as well.

She knew Annie just wasn't going to accept that without solid evidence.

"It's all a lot to take in, isn't it?" Annie pushed out her lower lip and blew upwards, making her pink fringe billow out from her forehead. "Okay, so where does that leave us? Are we any further forward than before?"

"I think we've just made a major step forward," said Charlie. "What was the last thing Pauline Wilson said before she left here last night?"

"Something about knowing Iris is innocent…"

"…and that she was planning to go to the police this morning!"

"Oh, Charlie, do you think that's why she was attacked?"

"Of course I do, Annie. And that tells us the real murderer was very likely to have been here in the bar last night when Pauline was having her say." She grabbed a pad of paper and pencil from behind the bar and seated herself at one of the tables, glancing at the clock at the same time. "Right, we've got about ten minutes before the lunchtime crowd start to arrive. Let's make a list of everyone who was in here at ten-thirty last night. I reckon we've got ourselves a much better suspect list!"

CHAPTER 27

It was a quiet lunchtime service, and by one-thirty there were just a couple of old-timers sitting in the corner of the bar putting the world to rights over the last of their pints. Charlie was happy to look after things on her own, so Annie changed into something slightly smarter than her usual jeans and tee-shirt before heading out of the pub and strolling across the green, past the church and down the road leading out of the village. The playground was empty as the kids were all back in their classrooms. After a few minutes, she turned right into a lane between two medieval thatched cottages, climbed the aptly if somewhat unimaginatively named Main Hill, passed through the stone gateway and approached the imposing edifice that was Mountjoy Manor. Climbing the steps to the front door, she raised the door knocker and let it fall gently back down. Within a few seconds, the door swung open. Expecting to be greeted by either Hilda Reynolds, or possibly a housekeeper, she was surprised to find herself face to face with the widow herself. She was impeccably turned out in a bright red tartan skirt and contrasting green blouse and cardigan. *Hardly widow's weeds,* thought Annie, then chided herself. Maybe customs were different where this woman came from. Ukraine, wasn't it? Annie held out her hand.

"Mrs Mountjoy, I'm Annie McLeod from The Falls."

The other woman nodded coolly and shook hands.

"Yes, I remember. You served our dinner last night. What can I do for you? Are you collecting for the jumble sale?"

"Goodness me, no," said Annie, shaking her head. "If you remember, you suggested I pop over and you'd show me around the house. Said you might be considering selling up?" She paused. "But if it's not convenient…"

At first, Olga seemed not to know what Annie was talking about, then her face cleared and she smiled.

"Of course! You told me you used to be an estate agent." She stood back and pointed into the hallway. "Please, do come in."

As Annie walked through the door, she paused and turned to Olga.

"I just wanted to tell you how sorry Charlie and I were about Mr Mountjoy's death."

"Thank you. Of course, Charlie was the one who found him, wasn't she?"

Closing the door, Olga led the way through the hallway to the back of the house.

As the two women stood in the centre of the kitchen-cum-dining room, Annie looked around with her professional eye. Taking in the combination of luxury and comfort, she knew if they lived here, her little family would rarely move from this room. And then she looked out of the window at the gardens swooping down to the stream with the hills in the background, and gasped.

"What a magnificent view!"

Olga glanced over her shoulder and smiled.

"Yes, it's beautiful, isn't it?"

"I thought we had a good view from the garden of The Falls, but this is something else. Are you a keen gardener, Mrs Mountjoy?"

"For goodness sake, call me Olga," she said, "Mrs Mountjoy makes me feel so old, like Simon's mother. I was

102

thinking of going back to my own name, but Perevernykruchenko is just too much of a mouthful. Next time, I'm going to marry a man called Smith!"

Annie stared at her silently, her shock obviously showing on her face, as the other woman laughed shrilly and Annie wondered if she'd been drinking.

"Look, Annie, I may call you Annie, yes? It's a pity my husband died, and I'm certainly sorry about how he died," she paused and pursed her lips, "but he's not the first person close to me I've lost through violence. It's getting to be a bit of a habit." She smiled then, the first genuine smile Annie had seen on her face. "But it's nice of you to call around like this. You're the only one who has, apart from the police, who have a job to do. Oh, and Anthony Farsider of course. I've seen an awful lot of Anthony this week." She opened a silver box on the coffee table, held it out to Annie who shook her head, then took out a long slim cigarette and lit it before continuing. "Now, would you like to see around the rest of the house?"

For the next half hour, Olga played at tour guide and Annie was genuinely impressed by everything she saw. From the kitchen area, they'd moved into the larger, more formal dining room.

"Simon used to host dinner parties for his business associates," said Olga. "And we used this a fair bit too," she went on, pointing to a small bar area decorated in dark greens, with leather Chesterfield sofas against two walls. They didn't visit the room to the right of the front door. "You know Hilda Reynolds, I'm sure? That's her domain. At least it is for now," Olga said in a quiet firm voice, but she wouldn't be drawn further.

Across the hallway from the office was the door into a large sunny room with windows on two sides.

"Simon always called this the drawing room," said Olga. "Apparently that's what his parents called it when they lived here during his childhood. It used to be kept for best – for entertaining special visitors like the vicar. But we used it in the evenings." More squashy sofas, this time in delicate pinks and yellows, lined the walls, while matching floor-length velvet curtains framed the windows on the front and side walls, plus the French door that led out into the garden. Annie thought it a wonderful mix of old world and new, the latter represented by a 54" screen on the wall opposite the front window.

The final room on the ground floor was much smaller. Decorated in blues and mauves, it contained a couple of easy chairs, a bookcase and a modest desk holding a compact looking laptop and a small printer. "This is where I spend my mornings," said Olga. "When I'm not in the pool, that is."

"You have a pool?" said Annie, innocently. "Wow, can I see it?"

Olga led the way back to the family room and through a small door in the side wall behind the seating area.

"This was a major change to the original house, of course," she said. "There were a few raised eyebrows at planning stage, but Simon managed to win them over. And you can't see it from the front, as there's a new shrubbery planted in front of it."

The pool room ran under the house and like the room above it, the back wall was completely made of glass. Towards the front of the house, Annie could see the shrubbery Olga referred to. It was a profusion of colours and made an effective screen.

"I swim here every morning," said Olga. "100 lengths each time." She smoothed her hands over her waist and hips, apparently proud of her figure. "And Nathan puts me through my paces in here as well."

"Wow, Suzy would love this," said Annie.

"Suzy? Who's Suzy?"

"Our daughter. You must have seen her at the barbecue party last weekend. She's eight, going on twenty-eight and loves swimming. Where we lived in London, she used to visit the local baths several times a week. But down here it's much harder, with the nearest pools being in Exeter or Newton Abbot. Of course, there's the open air one in Chudleigh during the summer. But Charlie and I are far too busy to take her more than a couple of times a month. And she's too young to go on her own yet."

"Well, she could always come here," said Olga.

"Oh, no, we couldn't…"

"Look, I told you, I use the pool every morning, but for the rest of the day it's just sitting here." She paused and stared out of the window for a long moment. When she looked back at Annie, there was a hint of a tear in her eye. "And it's about time we had the laughter of a child in this house."

"Well, if you're sure, that would be really good."

"Definitely. Look, there's a spare key to the outer door here somewhere." She looked around vaguely, then strolled over to a small shelf next to a glass door in the wall nearest the shrubbery. "You can come and go via this door, so you won't need to come into the house."

At that moment, a voice called from the kitchen above them.

"Olga darling, where are you…"

Nathan Williams strode down the stairs, wearing the briefest of swimming trunks. Beside her, she felt Olga freeze as she thrust the spare key into her hand.

"Look, I have to go now. Thank you for coming. Let me know what you think I should do about selling up. I'll show you the other parts of the house another time. But please do use the pool as often as you wish, any afternoon."

Annie glanced at the newcomer who was glaring at her. Then she turned back to Olga, thanked her for her time, repeated her condolences, and headed for the outside door. As she pulled it to behind her, she realised the lace on one of her trainers was undone, and bent down to retie it. The sound of raised voices reached her ear. She glanced back into the pool house. Olga had gone to join Nathan at the bottom of the staircase. And the two appeared to be arguing.

Annie took the path through the shrubbery and crossed the front of the house, heading for the gateway and the lane.

"Yessss!" she said softly to herself. "Mission accomplished." But, as she walked back towards the pub, she found herself thinking about Olga's truculent young trainer. He certainly didn't seem pleased with her at all. Why would it bother him if Olga had a visitor in her own home? Or was there some other reason the young man was annoyed? If Olga had been drinking in the morning, as Annie suspected, Nathan Williams was not going to be happy, was he? Maybe it was as simple as that.

CHAPTER 28

From behind his counter in Cosy Corner, Roger Richardson eyed his wife with suspicion and concern. Celia was not herself today. Hadn't been for the past couple of days in fact. Not that she wasn't hiding it well. She'd had her usual cheery smile and friendly word for everyone who came through the door. And she'd been on great form whenever Rohan had asked her a question or needed reminding where the refills for the condiments were kept.

But Roger had been an almost constant companion to Celia since the day they'd bonded over the sandpit in nursery school some forty years ago. He knew every inch of her face, every sign of her mood, every slight mannerism. And something was definitely not right. When no-one needed her attention, her eyes turned back to the window, and he had the distinct feeling she wasn't only in a different place, she was in a different time as well.

The café closed at four each day. The grocery store remained open until at least five-thirty, or sometimes later if there was a last-minute rush. Celia often popped into Chudleigh or Newton Abbot to get something special for tea. Then the couple would cook and eat their dinner as soon as Roger closed up. They both loved cooking and enjoyed sharing time in the kitchen, chatting over the day's events while preparing the meal.

So Roger wasn't surprised when Celia came down from the flat at just after four carrying her shopping bag. What did surprise him was she had changed into an emerald coloured dress and jacket instead of her more normal blouse and skirt. And she was wearing lipstick. Something was very definitely not right.

"Rohan, you couldn't do me a favour, could you?" Roger said, looking across at their new assistant who was sweeping the floor in the café.

"Sure, Roger, what do you need?"

"Will you keep an eye on the store for a few minutes? There's something I want to ask Celia to get for me. I'll just see if I can catch her before she drives off."

Leaving Rohan wandering across to the counter, Roger slipped out of the door and set off after his wife. There was no garage attached to Cosy Corner and the couple kept their car in one on Farm Lane, attached to the house of an elderly non-driving friend of Celia's mum. So Roger expected her to be walking past the school and across to the lane. But she was nowhere to be seen! How could she have disappeared so quickly? He'd only been a minute or so behind her.

Looking around wildly, he caught sight of a flash of green in the corner of his eye and was just in time to see his wife disappearing through the lych gate and into the churchyard. Without stopping to think, he set off in pursuit. He had a horrible suspicion he knew what he was going to see, and part of him desperately wanted to turn around and run back to the shop. If he didn't see it, it wouldn't really be happening. But the other part of him needed to know for sure.

It was Pauline Wilson who'd told him Stanley Wentworth was back. She'd heard someone talking about the grocery store on the new estate while she was helping with the church flowers. Someone mentioned the new manager used to live in the village but had been 'away' for a long time.

There were some sniggering comments about maybe he'd been 'at Her Majesty's pleasure' somewhere and she'd not really been paying attention, but then someone said his name was Stanley something and her ears pricked up. She'd remembered the name and how devastated Celia had been. Which is why she'd warned Roger.

The following day, he'd made the excuse of having to pop to the wholesaler for something and slipped out of the store just as the lunchtime rush was finishing. He'd taken the car, but instead of driving to Newton Abbot, had turned into the new estate and parked in one of the side roads. Strolling past the window of the new shop, he could see the manager talking to someone at the counter, and immediately knew Pauline's suspicions were correct. Stanley Wentworth was back in town, bold as brass. He was a bit heavier than before, carrying a bit of a paunch. His hair, what he had left of it, was salt and pepper rather than the glossy dark brown Roger remembered. But he still had the charming smile that used to make Celia blush. Roger had returned to Cosy Corner with slow dragging footsteps. He'd said very little for the rest of the afternoon, and it was mid-evening before he remembered he'd left the car parked on a side street and not in their garage where it should be.

Roger didn't tell Celia about Stanley's return, but he guessed someone else must have mentioned it because not long afterwards she started her window staring. When he asked her if she was alright, she said, yes of course. She was just a bit tired. They'd had a busy few weeks, with some outside catering events on top of all the baking and other work in the café, so he tried to believe her. But he wasn't convinced and his feeling of something terrible being about to happen had grown stronger over the past couple of days. And it looked as if he was right.

Now, making his way through the churchyard, dodging behind gravestones and overgrown shrubs, he finally spotted them. Sitting on the bench behind the church, talking urgently to one another. He slipped away, tears running down his face. When Celia returned home an hour and a half later with a full shopping bag, he couldn't face her. He said he had one of his migraines and was going to sleep it off.

CHAPTER 29: SATURDAY 13TH JULY

On Saturday morning Annie was at a loose end. With no overnight guests, there was no breakfast to prepare, apart from any walk-ins. And that was rare. Suzy had Youth Choir just after lunch, but wasn't likely to surface for a couple of hours yet. Saturday was the one day of the week she was allowed to set her own timetable. And Charlie was still planning the next week's meals ready for sending an order to the wholesaler.

"I think I'll just pop over to Cosy Corner," Annie said. "Do you want me to bring you anything?"

"One of Celia's cheese scones would be nice," was the reply from the back of the store cupboard.

"Okay, won't be long."

Celia was on her own. The breakfast rush was over and it was too early for lunch timers.

"No Roger today, Celia?" asked Annie as she stirred her coffee and contemplated treating herself to one of Celia's wonderful chocolate muffins.

"He's just popped out to the Post Office, lovey."

Annie grimaced.

"Ouch, Newton Abbot's going to be packed at this time on a Saturday, isn't it?" But Celia shook her head.

"Bless you, no. He's not gone to Newton. There's a post

office in the new grocery place up on the estate." Celia looked pensive for a moment or two, then sighed and carried on sorting stuff behind her gleaming counter.

Annie thought about this for a while. So, Roger was visiting the opposition, was he? Was he doing a spot of industrial espionage on the side? Or was there more to it than that?

"Tell me, Celia," she asked, "why was Roger so pleased to hear about Simon Mountjoy being killed?" As the words left her mouth, she realised there might have been a subtler way of approaching the subject, but it was too late now.

For a long moment, there was silence from the other woman. Then she picked up her coffee mug and came to join Annie in the otherwise empty café. She lowered herself into a chair and sighed.

"I'm rather sorry to say it's all my fault," she said. "The new place is run by someone we used to know years back. Someone I was very close to." She paused and bit her lip, stirring her coffee reflectively. "Roger and me were born within a couple of weeks of each other and have been friends since nursery school. We grew up together really. My parents were always busy running this place, so I spent more time at his house some years than at my own. Everyone, including us, assumed we'd get married in the end. But, when we were eighteen, Stanley Wentworth arrived in the village, and I'm afraid that was it, as far as I was concerned." She pulled a face. "It seems so daft now; but at the time, I couldn't think of anyone or anything but my Stanley. He was a bit older, see, and seemed so sophisticated. I'd planned to go to university, but that all went out the window. We got engaged the following Christmas and planned for a June wedding; I would have been just twenty."

"So what happened?"

"He left me! Disappeared in the April. Left no note, no explanation. Just went."

"Oh, Celia, that's terrible. You must have been devastated."

"I was, Annie. I was. It took me more than a year to get over it. I didn't come in here during opening hours for several months. I couldn't face people. Didn't want to see them laughing at me. Poor jilted Celia."

"Oh, I'm sure they wouldn't…"

"You're new to village life, aren't you, lovey?" Celia gave Annie a bleak smile. "There's a great sense of community. And most people are willing to help out in a crisis. But there's also an undercurrent of knowing everyone's business and judging people." She took another sip of coffee. "But eventually, I got up the courage to get back some sort of normality. And throughout it all, in the background, there was Roger. And we sort of slipped back into the old ways. And finally, when we were twenty-six, he walked me down the aisle. My parents were ready to retire, so we moved in upstairs and took over running this place." Then she looked up and smiled at Annie. "It was a bit of a shock when Stanley turned up here again, I can tell you. Roger thinks I don't know. Thinks he's protecting me. But I've known since the day he moved back."

"And did you ever find out why he disappeared?"

"Not really. There's a rumour he's been in prison. But to be honest, I don't really care."

Annie thought she saw a wistful look in Celia's eyes and wondered just what the other woman was really thinking. But then she had another thought.

"But I still don't understand the connection to Simon Mountjoy?"

"Ah, well, he financed the new place, you see. It's his fault all this blew up in the first place. When Roger heard about the plans, he went up to Mountjoy Manor to have it out with Simon. Apparently, it started off amicably enough, but got quite heated and Simon ended up throwing Roger out." She gave a bit of a giggle. "If it wasn't so serious, it would be quite amusing. The thought of two grown men arguing like kids in the schoolyard." Then her smile faded. "But of course, it's not funny. Not funny at all."

"Bad for business?" asked Annie.

"You could say that. It's not desperate yet, but we have to keep ahead of the tricks they're playing up there. Roger's been plotting against Simon Mountjoy and his grocery shop ever since. And when he found out who Simon had employed as the new manager, that just made things worse." She drained her mug and stood up, smiling down at Annie as she did so. "But only in a business sense, you realise. I know what you're thinking. But my Roger could never hurt a fly."

CHAPTER 30

"I still can't believe you managed to get access to Mountjoy Manor so easily," said Charlie, as she and Annie stood in the doorway watching Suzy walk around the village green and through the lych gate into the churchyard. "Now we can have a proper nose around."

"Oh no we can't, Charlie Jones!" said Annie, putting her hands on her hips and shaking her head. "We've got permission to use the pool room only! We won't be going anywhere near the rest of the house. I suspect the door into the kitchen will be locked, anyway." She paused and shrugged. "That's if Olga doesn't change her mind and stop us from visiting at all. That trainer of hers didn't look at all happy when he saw me yesterday." But Charlie waved away her objections.

"Phooey. She's not going to take the key away now she's given it to us. And she's the lady of the manor, not some jumped-up trainer." She grinned and nodded her head. "You mark my words. Once we've been there a few times, we'll be accepted as part of Olga's circle of friends. We'll soon be able to find out what's been going on in that house."

"Her circle of friends, is it, Charlie? I'm not sure that's a particularly large group from what she implied yesterday.

She thanked me for making the effort to go and see her, when no-one else has."

"Come on, Annie, where's your spirit of adventure? Aren't you excited at the chance of swimming in the big house?" She framed the last two words with her fingers as she said it. "I know Suzy is. She was delighted when I told her where we'd be going after she gets back from Youth Choir." She pulled Annie towards her and popped a kiss on the end of her nose. "Right, I'm off to The Folly to find my swimming costume. Do you want me to get yours as well?"

Annie sighed and then grinned.

"Yes please, Charlie. I must admit, it'll be quite nice to get back in the water after all this time."

But before Charlie could disappear through the back door, DCI Harolds and DS Smith walked in. The pair ordered coffees and prepared to take them over to a table in the window.

"Any news on Pauline?" asked Annie as she handed over their change. The DCI nodded her head.

"Yes, there is. I'm pleased to say Ms Wilson has recovered consciousness. She's still woozy and very confused. She hasn't been able to tell us what happened. But the doctor says that's natural in the circumstances. He reckons she should be much better in the morning. If there's no deterioration in her condition, he's going to let us interview her as soon as he's finished his ward rounds."

"Well, that is good news," said Annie. She turned around. "Did you hear that, Charlie…?" But Charlie was nowhere to be seen. "Well, how strange. Where's she got to?"

"There she is," said DS Smith, pointing out of the window, "she's outside." Annie was surprised to see Charlie standing in the car park outside the pub looking in both directions. Then she shrugged and disappeared back around the side of the building. A few moments later, she appeared at Annie's side behind the bar once more.

"Where did you get to?" asked Annie. "One minute you

were there and the next…"

"I heard something – or someone. Just as the DCI was telling us about Pauline coming round. Annie, I think there was someone in the corridor listening at the inner door. That's why I went outside to have a look. But by the time I got there, the corridor was empty. And there was no-one on the street that I could see."

"Oh, you're probably hearing things."

"Maybe I am, Annie. You could be right." Charlie paused and pulled a face. "But I think, just to be on the safe side, I'm going to have a word with DCI Harolds. I'd never forgive myself if anything else happened to Pauline. And we don't know if anyone's told her what Pauline said in here on Thursday night, do we?"

She put down the glass she'd been polishing and started to cross the bar. Just at that moment, the phone rang. It was the wholesalers with a query about the order she'd placed earlier that day. And by the time she'd finished with her call, the two detectives had left.

CHAPTER 31

In the event, Annie didn't go swimming with them after all. She had a call from a rep who was in the area and wanted to call in at The Falls on his way past.

"You go, Charlie," she said. "I saw the place yesterday. I can come next time. One of us needs to stay here, but we don't both need to see this guy. And Suzy will be disappointed if she misses her treat."

Youth Choir finished at half past three. Quite often it was closer to four o'clock by the time Suzy had finished chatting to her friends or their parents and arrived back at the pub. But today she was on the doorstep within three minutes of the choir master declaring the rehearsal over.

"Wow, you must have been standing by the door ready to run," said Annie. "Go on, off you go, the pair of you. It's hard to tell which of you is the most excited!"

Charlie blew her a kiss and then held the door open for Suzy.

"Ready for the big adventure then, Suzy?"

When they reached the gates of Mountjoy Manor, Suzy suddenly hung back, apparently overawed by the size and grandeur of the place. Charlie took her hand and pulled her gently towards the shrubbery on the right of the building.

"Come on, poppet, it's fine," she said. "It's not as

though we'll be trespassing. We've been invited, remember." As they reached the bushes, she pointed to a narrow gravel pathway skirting the lilac and elder. "This way; Mummy Annie said it was just behind here."

They found the glass door straight away and let themselves into the pool room.

"Wow," said Suzy, "Mummy Annie wasn't kidding, was she?"

"Not bad. Not bad at all." Charlie looked around for a changing room, but realised there wasn't going to be one. "They probably get dressed in the house and then stroll through. Good job we put our swimsuits on under our clothes, isn't it, Suzy?"

The pair stripped off and quickly entered the clear blue water. It was a tad chilly to start with, but a couple of lengths soon warmed them up. Suzy had been a keen swimmer in London and easily kept up with her mother. In fact, she passed her on the final few yards and let out a yell of triumph, hastily silenced as Charlie pretended to chase her, threatening a ducking.

For the next hour they alternated between practising their lengths and playing tag and ball in the water. Then they climbed out and stretched themselves on a couple of loungers to dry off. The sun shone through the huge expanse of glass, warming the air and making them feel as if they were sunbathing in the Mediterranean.

Charlie kept glancing at the door into the main house. Occasionally she thought she heard movement or voices, but the door stayed resolutely closed. Finally, she glanced at the ornate clock on the wall and jumped up.

"Come on, Suzy, it's turned five. Mummy Annie will have dinner ready and she'll be cross if we're late!" They pulled their clothes back on, Suzy pulling a face at the feel of wet costume under her tee-shirt.

They pulled the outside door closed behind them. Charlie locked it carefully and popped the key in her jeans pocket, then they headed back through the shrubbery and into the front garden.

"What on earth's going on? Why are you trespassing?" A loud voice startled them and they looked towards the window of the lounge. It was wide open and Nathan Williams was standing glaring at them. "This is private property, you know!" he went on.

Suzy grabbed Charlie's hand and hid behind her. Charlie raised her other hand in a mock salute.

"Hello, Nathan. Goodness, you startled us. We're not trespassing. Annie called to see Olga yesterday and she kindly gave us an open invitation to use the pool any afternoon." She took the key out of her pocket and held it up. "See, we have a key and everything. We've had a lovely swim, haven't we, Suzy?"

"Oh, okay, well, she didn't tell me, but in that case, I guess it's okay. Sorry to have made you jump." Nathan closed the window with a sharp click. As the pair continued on their way towards the gates, Charlie felt a prickle between her shoulder blades. She threw a quick glance back towards the house. Sure enough, Olga Mountjoy's personal trainer was standing at the window, staring at them.

"So you had a good time," said Annie later, as they sat down to ham salad and fresh bread. Suzy nodded.

"Definitely. I hope we can go every day!" She paused and scratched her head. "But I certainly hope we don't see that horrid man again. He was really scary."

CHAPTER 32

By five o'clock, Roger felt like an over-tightened spring that was about to pop. He'd walked back to the new estate that morning to collect his car and, on the way, had called into the grocery store. Stanley Wentworth had been working in the office at the back and hadn't looked up. Roger didn't know whether he was pleased about that or not. He would dearly love to challenge this man who disrupted their lives so drastically all those years ago and looked as if he was back for a repeat performance. But on the other hand, he wasn't sure he could trust himself not to hit him. And Roger knew he was no fighter. He'd bought a newspaper and left.

Celia had barely spoken a word to him all day. It wasn't that she was being unfriendly. She'd responded to all his questions and comments. She'd laughed when he'd made a joke with one of the customers. And she'd saved one of her precious pasties and shared it with him at lunchtime. But he couldn't shake the feeling she was waiting for the right moment to tell him something.

As they sat in the lounge after finishing supper and stacking the dishwasher, Roger stared out of the window. The evening sun had disappeared behind a bank of black cloud. It seemed to sum up how he was feeling and he could stand it no longer.

"Celia, love, I know Stanley Wentworth's back in the village. Are you having an affair?"

Celia gasped at him, then put her head in her hands. Her shoulders began to heave. Roger felt the room spin. He'd been right. What was he going to do? He couldn't live without her. Then, she raised her head and he saw her eyes were crinkled with amusement.

"You are a daft bugger, Roger Richardson. Don't you know by now, you're the only one I love. And if I was going to have an affair, which I'm not, Stanley Wentworth would be the last man I would look at."

"But I saw you, yesterday, in the churchyard…"

"He's been pestering me since he came back. I've been trying to ignore him. I didn't want to worry you with it. But on Wednesday night he pushed a note through the letter box begging me to meet him. Said he wanted to explain!"

"And did he?"

"Sort of. He admitted he'd been a bit of a bad boy in the past, before he came to the village, before he met me. He swore he'd gone straight once we got together. But someone tipped him the wink his past was about to catch up with him. Hence the reason he did a runner."

"Sounds a bit weak to me, love."

"Me too, Roger. Me too. So I told him in no uncertain terms I didn't want to see him ever again, and that he's not welcome at Cosy Corner." She smiled at him ruefully. "But I'm a bit worried about his reaction. He swore he's going all out to ruin us as a result. I didn't know how to tell you, Roger."

At that moment, the sun crept out from behind the cloud bank and lit up the room and its occupants. Roger let out a deep sigh and grabbed Celia's hand.

"Well if that's all we've got to worry about, Celia, I think we're going to be fine. We've faced worse than this together. And don't forget, Stanley Wentworth was being bankrolled by Simon Mountjoy. Now he's no longer with us, I suspect life might not be quite so easy for the new grocery store and its manager."

CHAPTER 33

Charlie looked up as the door opened a little after seven and Anthony and Marion Farsider walked in. He was wearing a navy blazer, tan trousers and what looked to her like a regimental tie. She was elegant and classy in a little black number that Charlie was pretty sure hadn't come from Marks & Spencer. They looked like a prosperous couple out for a night on the town and Charlie wondered just why they were spending their evening in a country pub, rather than a posh restaurant in Exeter. But then again, The Falls was in walking distance of the Farsider residence. Maybe that was it. She jumped when Annie tapped her on the shoulder and whispered.

"Oh, yes, I forgot to tell you, Charlie, Anthony phoned while you were at the pool with Suzy. He wanted to make sure we hadn't forgotten about his booking for this evening. Seems like there's something to celebrate. Do you want me to see to them?"

"No, it's okay, I'll do it. You stay in the bar. And when I get back, you can remind me again why we agreed to give Rohan the evening off on a Saturday." Charlie walked across the room and pinned a welcoming smile on her face. "Good evening, Marion, Anthony. Let me show you to your table."

"Capital, capital," the little man said, following her

across the room. His wife trailed behind him. As the pair settled themselves at the secluded corner table, Charlie grabbed some menus and handed them out. Anthony took his but put it to one side. "Plenty of time for that later. First, a bottle of your finest champagne!"

Charlie opened her eyes wide and stared at him.

"I'm not sure we have much in the way of bubbly, Anthony."

"When I checked with Annie this afternoon, I specifically told her we were celebrating and needed something decent waiting on ice. She said it would be no problem." A frown start to appear on the man's face. "You're not going to let me down, are you?"

"Of course not, Anthony." Charlie took a deep breath. "I'll just go and check in the wine cellar."

She hurried down the stairs to the dark little alcove she had jokingly labelled the wine cellar when they took over the pub. Annie popped her head over the bannister.

"Psst, Charlie. There's a bottle at the very back." She paused and smiled ruefully. "I bought it as a surprise, keeping it for your birthday next month, but I guess I can always buy another one."

Charlie grabbed the bottle, impressed at Annie's gesture and even more so at her choice, then ran back up the stairs. She dropped a kiss on Annie's cheek as she passed her by.

"Here you are, Anthony, one special bottle just for you and Marion. It's quite chilled already, but I'll just put it in an ice bucket for a while…"

But he waved his hands impatiently at her.

"Just open the thing, Charlie, just open it!"

"So, celebrating, are you?" asked Charlie as she smoothly opened the bottle and poured two foaming flutes.

"We certainly are. The deal is settled. As soon as Simon's probate goes through, Farsider-Mountjoy Developments Ltd will no longer be my responsibility." He reached across and patted his wife's hand. "And we can finally get on with the rest of our lives."

Marion Farsider smiled back at her husband and then looked up rather shyly at Charlie.

"I've not been too well for a while now, Charlie. It looks like it's been all sorted out for the moment, but it's made us realise how short life is and that we shouldn't let work get in the way of living. Anthony has promised we can do some travelling now he's stepping back from the business. I've always wanted to go on a cruise."

"And so you shall, my dear," said her husband, taking a deep swig from his glass. "So you shall. We're going to do things in style from now on."

"A good deal then, is it?" asked Charlie, as she handed them the menus once more and took out her pad and pencil.

"Absolutely. I think it's fair to say our money worries are over and we're going to be living it up from now on. Two and a half million they've agreed to pay for the company."

"Not that we're getting all the money, of course," said his wife. Charlie wondered if she was quite as comfortable with all this as her husband. He chuckled.

"Yes, that's right – although even a mill and a bit isn't to be sniffed at." He pointed up the road in the direction of Mountjoy Manor. "I reckon Madam at the big house will be smiling tonight as well. She's going to have a lot more liquid assets than she expected. Very much the Merry Widow, I reckon she'll be."

"Hush now, Anthony, that's not a nice way to talk about Olga. Simon's only been dead a few days. She's bound to be upset."

Anthony snorted and winked at Charlie. "Always the charitable one, my wife," he said indulgently. "We were with them, you know, for lunch. On Sunday?"

"Really?" Charlie wondered just how much this man would be willing to say if pushed gently. "It was a business lunch, then?"

"Sort of. The film crew had finished work on that TV programme about the renovation of Mountjoy Manor and Simon invited them to lunch before they headed back to

London."

"Oh, so nothing to do with selling the business then?"

"No, no. In fact at that point, I wasn't sure if the deal would go through or not. I'd got it all sorted out in principle with the guys in London, only to find Simon wasn't half as keen on the whole idea as I'd thought he was. He didn't exactly turn it down, but he kept finding all sorts of excuses for not giving his agreement. Our buyers were a bit fed up, as you'd imagine, and they'd given me an ultimatum. Either agree the contract by the end of this week or the whole thing was off. I was furious with Simon and meant to sort it all out with him on the Monday, but in the end, I never got the chance to talk to him."

"But you said the deal's going through now?" said Charlie.

"Well, yes. I went up to see Olga earlier in the week and again yesterday afternoon. I put on a bit of a charm offensive, and persuaded her to sell. Actually, it wasn't that difficult. She's not interested in business, but she's definitely interested in money. And she'll need a fair bit of that if she's going to keep Mountjoy Manor up and running now she's on her own." Pausing for breath and taking another swig from his glass, Anthony finally turned his attention to the menu. "Right, let's get our food ordered, shall we? Otherwise, the kitchen's going to be closed."

Much later, after everyone had gone and the clearing up was finished, Charlie and Annie pulled out their suspect list from the previous night.

"Well, I guess that confirms a couple of names on our list," said Charlie.

"What, both Anthony and his wife?"

"Well Anthony's on there already. But, no, I wasn't talking about Marion. She struck me as much too timid to ever kill anyone and get away with it. No, I was thinking about the Merry Widow as Anthony referred to her."

"Okay, so Anthony and Olga are on the list. What about

Olga's handsome personal trainer?"

"Not too sure about him to be honest. We'll keep our ears to the ground, but I suspect he's just after whatever he can get from his current position."

CHAPTER 34

As Charlie and Annie put away their list and prepared to head off to bed, there was a hammering on the front door. Charlie strode over and unbolted it. She was surprised to see Hilda Reynolds on the doorstep. But this wasn't the efficient executive assistant everyone was used to seeing organising Simon Mountjoy's life. Nor was it the composed woman who two nights ago had told Charlie she believed Iris to be innocent. Now, the woman's hair was straggling out of its usual French pleat and her eyes were red, as though she'd had been crying. Charlie grabbed her arm and pulled her into the bar.

"Ms Reynolds, Hilda, what on earth is it? Are you okay?"

"You haven't been attacked, too, have you?" said Annie, rushing to her side. But their visitor shook her head.

"No, no, it's nothing like that. I've just had the most tremendous row with Olga—Mrs Mountjoy. And I think I need your help! Or at least, Iris does."

A few minutes later, the three were settled in a semi-circle around one of the tables in the empty restaurant, each nursing a mug of Charlie's hot chocolate complete with a shot of brandy. Charlie turned to their visitor.

"Right, let's hear it, Ms Reynolds. What's the problem and what can we do to help?"

Their visitor took a deep breath and put her cup down.

"Hilda will do just fine," she said. "Now, you've probably guessed I've known Iris Murphy for longer than the few months she's been here in Coombesford?" Charlie and Annie nodded but said nothing, not wanting to interrupt the other woman's flow. "In fact, I've known her since she was eight years old. Although she wasn't called Iris Murphy then. Her real name is Lily Fitzgibbons-Mountjoy."

"She's Simon's daughter?" asked Charlie.

"Stepdaughter actually. Her mother was Angela, Simon's first wife." She paused and bit her lip. "Angela died in a tragic accident while Simon was away on a business trip. She was an alcoholic. Hit by a car one afternoon while blind drunk. Lily was just seventeen at the time. She blamed her stepfather for her mother's death."

"Why would she do that?"

"I'm afraid Simon wasn't as discreet with his flings as he liked to think he was. Angela's drinking only started after they married and got worse every time he had an affair."

"So Lily left home?" said Annie gently. Hilda nodded.

"Yes, she ran away on the day of her mother's funeral and we never heard from her again. At least, that's what Simon believed." She paused and sipped her drink. "I made Lily promise she would keep in touch with me, so I'd know she was all right. And she kept that promise. Then earlier this year, she phoned me and said she was ready to confront her stepfather. Said she was coming to Coombesford, but begged me not to say anything. She wanted to do things her own way."

"So when she applied for the chef's job here…"

"…it was at my suggestion, yes. I knew you were looking for staff and it would mean she'd be close at hand."

"And when did she break the news to her stepfather that she was back in town?" asked Annie. "I take it he didn't recognise her at first?"

"That's right. The smart, slim woman she's become bears little resemblance to the overweight teenager with cropped, black hair and glasses that ran away all those years ago. She only told him on the day he died. She didn't warn me she was coming up to the house, so it was a real surprise when she appeared during the lunch party."

"And did you hear the argument they had?"

"They were shouting so loud, I'm surprised half the village didn't hear them." Hilda gave a rueful smile. "I went through to the front of the house to see what was going on, and Olga followed me. We were standing in the hall when the office door flew open and Lily came flying out. I put my arms out to grab hold of her, but she shook me off. 'Not now, Hilda,' she said and ran out of the door."

Charlie had been keeping quiet so far, but now she gave a gentle cough.

"You realise what this means, don't you?" she said. "Iris might have a motive for killing Simon Mountjoy. I wonder if the police know who she really is?"

"Well, if they don't yet, they will very soon," Hilda said. "That's what my row with Olga was about. Apparently she's been going through some of Simon's papers and suddenly realised who Iris is. And she's guessed I knew all along. She's saying this proves Iris killed Simon and I helped her. She's given me the sack!" The woman bit her lip and then started crying once more.

"Oh, Hilda, that's awful," said Annie, putting her arm around the older woman's shoulders. "What are you going to do?"

Hilda wiped her eyes and gave Annie a watery smile.

"Oh, I'm not bothered about me, Annie. I was going to retire when I'd sorted things out at Mountjoy Manor anyway. Simon left me well cared for in his will—and even if Olga contests that, I've got my apartment in Exeter and my savings. I'll be fine."

"But you're worried about Iris," said Charlie. "You think this is going to make the case against her even stronger, don't you?"

Hilda nodded.

"Exactly."

"Hilda, I have to ask this. What makes you so certain Iris didn't kill Simon?" Annie gave a gasp, but Charlie held up her hand. "No, Annie, I know you believe Iris is innocent, but belief isn't going to be enough. Is there any proof?" She looked across at the other woman. "Hilda?"

"Because, Charlie, she was with me at the time he was killed," said Hilda. "When I left Mountjoy Manor an hour or so after the row, Simon was alive. He waved to me from the kitchen as I left. I found Iris standing on the side of the main road, trying to hitch a lift. I drove her into Exeter; we had a bite to eat and then I left her at the bus station. I begged her to stay with me, at least for the night, but she was adamant she didn't want to remain in Devon any longer." She shrugged her shoulders. "But who's going to believe me? I've been lying for her for years."

"You said you dropped her at the bus station?" asked Charlie. "Do we know which bus she got?"

"Well, she eventually ended up in Birmingham. That's where the police found her. But I suspect she stopped off somewhere else on the way. It was nearly eight by the time I left her at the bus station. There weren't that many options on a Sunday night. But the police aren't going to believe us, are they? We need some independent witnesses." She paused and then went on. "But that's not the only thing that's concerning me. There's still a murderer somewhere around here. And if Pauline Wilson's attack is connected with Simon's death, as seems likely, then that murderer is still probably in the village. We need to find out who it is for everyone's safety."

Charlie had long since taught Annie the art of non-verbal conversations, something she'd honed as a child with her sister Suzanne when they were in trouble with their parents. Now, she glanced across at her wife and read the same level of trust in her eyes she herself was feeling towards the older woman. She nodded and smiled.

"Okay, Hilda, it looks like we need to work together on

this. Annie and I have been doing a bit of nosing around and we think we've come up with a list of suspects."

The two women ran through the thoughts they'd already had. Hilda agreed with their findings, but in the end they were no closer to working out who the culprit was.

"Charlie, look at the time! We need to get back to The Folly," said Annie. She turned to Hilda to explain. "Iris is babysitting tonight, and she'll be wondering where we are. And, Hilda, you're welcome to stay here tonight. There's plenty of room upstairs."

"How about we all go to see Iris then?" said Charlie. "I think we need another set of eyes on this and it's time she told us the full story."

CHAPTER 35

Iris was curled up in the upstairs lounge of The Folly, dozing over a book. Charlie and Annie made fresh drinks while Iris and Hilda hugged and brought each other up to date on recent events.

"Well, you've had an interesting time over the past few years, haven't you?" asked Charlie when they were all finally settled, their drinks in front of them.

"You might say that." Iris nodded. "But all the time, I wanted to come back here and talk to Simon. It felt so much like unfinished business, you know?"

"Of course I do. It's only natural. You were very close to your mother?"

"Absolutely. My real dad abandoned us the day I was born. They had a fight; he hit Mum and disappeared from the flat. He took all his stuff while we were still in hospital and by the time we got 'home' he was back home in America. We never heard from him or saw him throughout my childhood. There was some legal stuff to go through, but to all intents and purposes, I was the child of an unmarried mother.

"According to Mum, those first few weeks in the flat in London were pretty grim. We had very little money and she struggled to look after me. One evening, when she had no money for food for herself, and she was having difficulty feeding me, she swallowed her pride and used the phone box at the bottom of the stairs to phone her parents. And that's when my life really began.

"Grandpops and Granny were absolutely lovely. I adored them, and the feeling was mutual. Apparently, they jumped in the car as soon as Mum called them and drove up to collect us. They hadn't been too happy about the way she'd married in secret and kept a lot of things, including my birth, from them, but they never threw it in her face.

"We lived in this big old house on the edge of a town. Grandpops was a vet and he used to take me with him sometimes when he was visiting his patients. There were always stray cats, dogs or birds in the house – and once we even had a little lamb to look after. I would rush home from nursery to see it and help Granny with the feeding.

"When I was four, Mum got herself a job, and Granny started meeting me from nursery and looking after me pretty much full time. That was absolutely the best time ever and I'm sure I was more than a bit spoiled by her. After two years, we rented a flat in town, closer to where Mum was working, and also to give her a bit of independence, she said. I was sad to have to leave Granny and Grandpops behind, but we still went to visit them most weekends, so it wasn't too bad.

"We weren't living in the flat for very long, as this was also the time Mum met Simon Mountjoy. He had lots of money and was very good at spending it on people. Mum got flowers and chocolates all the time. I got toys and records and lots of other things. I tried to be nice to him for Mum's sake, but I could see he didn't really like me that much and he would really have been much happier if I didn't exist. But I did, so he had to put up with me. He wanted Mum, and I was part of the package.

"To be honest, as time went on, I got to quite like him, and gradually we learned to live together more or less happily. The wedding was great fun; and I was such a brat,

I really enjoyed being the centre of attention. I even hoped people would remember the flower girl in the pale blue taffeta dress with real flowers in her hair, even more than they remembered the bride or groom.

"We left our little flat in Guildford and moved to his place in Hammersmith. It was really posh and I had a huge room of my own with its own bathroom – or the en suite as Simon taught me to call it. I think Mum was a bit intimidated by it all to start with, but we settled in pretty well. I went to a nearby prep school and later to a private secondary school. And things went along pretty well until I was in my late teens."

Iris stared into the middle distance and the others said nothing. After a few moments she shook herself and smiled ruefully at them.

"The phone call came in the middle of the afternoon. I remember it was a Wednesday, as we were nearing the end of double science. I had to go to the head's office and I knew something terrible had happened before she even opened her mouth. It was the way she told me to sit down and took my hand, looking at me with those big, hang-dog eyes of hers. It was the same look I'd seen on Granny's face when she had to tell me a favourite puppy had died.

"Everyone was so kind to me, but it all went over my head to a great extent. I insisted I should be the one to ring Simon. And against their better judgment, they went along with my request. I'd got the number of the hotel from his office and by the time I rang, it was the middle of the night in Moscow. Luckily the receptionist spoke good English and put me straight through to his room. Except it wasn't Simon who answered. It was some bitch with an Australian accent! But I knew it was the right room, as she handed the phone straight over to him.

"The time leading up to the funeral was horrendous. Granny and Grandpops tried really hard to be brave for my sake, but I could see they were really broken up inside. And every time someone said how much I looked like my mum,

I could see it brought back more memories for them. I knew I couldn't stay with them. And as for going back to stay with Simon, that was never on the cards. Any feelings I'd had for him evaporated when I realised he'd been cheating on Mum. Suddenly the drinking and the final moments of her life made a lot more sense. The official result of the inquest was accidental death while under the influence of excess alcohol. Simon once suggested Mum might have done it deliberately, and blamed himself. Well, he'd got that right. I was sure Mum didn't mean to kill herself, but the fact she was in that state at all was certainly down to him.

"I was nearly eighteen by then, so it was perfectly legal for me to live on my own. The police won't chase after a runaway of that age. I prepared carefully. I had quite a lot of money in my savings account. Certainly enough to keep me going until I could find myself a job. I withdrew it all over the course of a few days, and stashed it where no-one would find it. And Simon had paid for driving lessons and bought me a car as soon as I turned seventeen. I slipped away during the wake, driving off with a couple of bags, and all my money, while everyone was drinking Mum's health. Ironic really considering how she died. I never made contact with Simon again, although I sent an occasional card to my grandparents to let them know everything was fine.

"I needed to get as far away as possible from London and Simon. I didn't want anyone to see me and tell him where I was. So I pointed the car north and crossed the border into Scotland the following morning after stopping overnight in a tiny bed and breakfast place in Northumbria. I looked quite mature for my age and the landlady was happy to accept my money and give me a cosy room and a wonderful breakfast in return.

"I finally stopped driving and running when I reached Fort William. There was always plenty of work there, especially around holiday season, and I settled in quite quickly.

"I changed my name right from the start, so there was

no chance of my being found unless I wanted to be. The little flower girl was all grown up now, but I still wanted to keep a link with the old me, so I became Iris Murphy, and constructed a whole new back story for myself in case anyone asked. Not that anyone ever did, to be honest.

"I worked in the hotel trade from then on; starting as a chambermaid and gradually working my way up to receptionist and functions manager in a small family-run place. Then one day, a chance offer to help out in a crisis changed my life. We had a big function on, and the kitchen was short-staffed. I offered to help, walked into that hectic behind-the-scenes world and was hooked. I applied to catering college, finished my initial training and then headed off to get some real world experience. I won't go into how I managed to get a passport, as it may not have strictly been legal, but I managed it through one of the contacts I'd made in the hotel. It's amazing what you can get hold of if you know who to ask."

CHAPTER 36

The meeting finally broke up just before one-thirty. Iris offered to walk Hilda back to the main building and get her settled in one of the empty bedrooms.

Annie was already in bed, and Charlie was just about to join her, when a sudden thought hit her.

"Pauline! My God! Pauline Wilson!"

"What about her?" said Annie, sitting up in bed in alarm.

"I forgot to tell Harolds about this morning's intruder."

"If it was an intruder, that is. You could have been hearing things!"

"But supposing I wasn't hearing things? Supposing it was the real murderer listening at the door? The one who attacked Pauline? Supposing they heard DCI Harolds say she was awake and she was going to interview her tomorrow morning?" She turned and looked at Annie. "Don't you see? Tonight's the only chance they'll have to silence Pauline once and for all. And she's all alone in that hospital!"

"Of course she's not alone, Charlie. She's in a private room in a private hospital with medical staff all around her."

"Yes, but she's in danger!" Charlie sat on the bed and started tying the laces on her trainers. Then she jumped up, grabbed her jacket from the back of the door and looked around wildly for her car keys. "Get on the phone now,

Annie. Phone the police and tell them they need to get someone over to the hospital right away. Tell them to contact Harolds and Smith. They'll understand. At least, you'll have to make them understand."

She headed for the door.

"Charlie." Annie's voice stopped her in her tracks. "Where are you going, Charlie?"

"I'm going to the hospital of course, Annie. I can be there much quicker than anyone else. If anything happens to Pauline, I'd never forgive myself."

The car started first time, and Charlie pulled out onto the dark lane, her raised headlights spotlighting into the sky. Within seconds, she was turning onto the A38, deserted at this time of night apart from an occasional lorry heading for Plymouth and the ferry terminal. The journey of fifteen miles took Charlie slightly less than ten minutes to complete and she was thankful the rural police force wasn't out patrolling the roads tonight.

She pulled into the car park outside the small private hospital, left the car in a space normally reserved for the chief consultant, and dashed through the main doors. There was no-one behind the reception desk, although she could hear the murmur of voices in the distance.

"Wilson, Pauline Wilson," she muttered to herself, leaning over the desk and pulled a typed sheet towards her. She found her name halfway down the list. "Room 27!" A sign on the wall told her rooms 21 to 28 were on the second floor. Running to the lift, she hit the up button. A light above the door illuminated 3, and stayed there. Turning away, she launched herself towards the stairs, taking them two at a time. By the time she reached the second landing, she was puffing and stopped to bend over and ease her breathing. "Boy, but you're getting out of shape, Charlie," she told herself. "You need to get back into training." Looking around, she saw a corridor leading away from the landing, with closed doors on each side. The one to the left was labelled 21, and to the right, 22. She raced down the corridor and stopped outside the fourth door on the left. Pausing, she peered through the glass panel in the door. Pauline Wilson was sleeping in the hospital bed, a faint night light on the bedside stand. She looked peaceful and content. Charlie breathed a sigh of relief, thinking she'd made a mistake. But at that moment, a figure detached itself from the corner of the room and glided towards the bed. The figure was wearing the white coat of a doctor, and carrying a pillow. A pillow which it appeared to be holding over Pauline Wilson's head.

"We need some help in here," screamed Charlie, then threw the door open. The figure spun around, dropped the pillow and surged towards her, throwing a wild punch in her direction. But she'd been in this game too long for that. Stepping swiftly to one side, she avoided the fist, while positioning her feet to trip the fleeing person. The pair fell to the floor with a bang. Charlie slid against the wall, while her assailant's head smashed into the side of a trolley in the corner of the room. There was a terrific clatter. Pauline Wilson opened her eyes and screamed. Charlie heard running feet and two nurses dashed into the room.

"What the hell's going on in here?" said one of them, reaching for the light switch. The overhead neon strips momentarily blinded Charlie. When she could see again, she found herself staring at the prone figure across the room from her. It was Olga Mountjoy's personal trainer, Nathan Williams.

The prostrate man groaned and opened his eyes. He attempted to jump up, but Charlie was too quick for him and pushed him back down against the wall.

"Oh no, you don't," she said. And as she heard police sirens in the distance, she began to relax for the first time since she'd been in the bedroom with Annie. "There are some people on their way to see you, young man. You've got some explaining to do!"

CHAPTER 37: SUNDAY 14TH JULY

"I understand you've waived your right to a solicitor, Mr Williams?" DCI Harolds looked across the table at the man slumped in the chair opposite. He just shrugged and nodded his head. "Although, we've had a chat with our colleagues at HMRC who looked you up on the National Insurance database, but couldn't find any record of a Nathan Williams living and working in this part of the world. Do you want to start by telling us who you really are?"

The man looked up and stared silently at the detectives for a while, chewing the side of his index finger. Then he shrugged again and started speaking, quietly at first, his voice getting stronger as he went on.

"My name's Nathan Hughes. My father was Ellis Hughes, an engineer. He worked for the same electronics company as Simon Mountjoy back in the 1980s."

Harolds glanced at DS Smith who was seated next to her, and raised her eyebrows.

"And what brought you to Devon, Mr Hughes? And why were you trying to kill Pauline Wilson?"

"I did my degree at Exeter University, in sports science. When I graduated, I went home to Wales. But it was too quiet for me, and Mum has her own set of friends now she's a widow. So I came back to Devon a couple of years ago. I was living in Exeter and working as a trainer in a gym on the outskirts of the city. And it was there, one day last June, I saw Simon Mountjoy for the second time in my life. The first time was when I was a child."

"What was the connection between your father and Simon Mountjoy? Apart from working in the same company, that is."

"Dad was a dreamer, an inventor. From the time he could write, he was always designing bits and pieces. His notebooks, which go back to his teenage years, are packed with designs for gadgets to make life easier for people in the house or in the workplace. But unfortunately, he never got any of them past the drawing board. Except one. But then his dream was taken away from him. That killed him in the end.

"Simon had come down to Wales for a meeting with Dad and took us all out for a drive and lunch in a country pub. He was the perfect host and tried hard to make friends with my mother, but I could tell she didn't trust him. It was only later I discovered exactly how he was to blame for my poor father's death.

"Dad was four years younger than Simon. When he joined the company, he was just twenty-seven and Simon was in a middle management position. Dad was in the engineering team, working on new product development. He worked long hours on behalf of that company. But at weekends and late into the evenings during the summer, he worked on his own projects.

"Dad and Simon bonded over a love of old American cars. Simon had a 1950s Corvette he'd shipped over from the States. Dad heard him talking about it one day and asked if he could have a look. Simon had been trying to find a particular spare part but with no success. So Dad made one for him, just like that. And a friendship was cemented. Well, as much as Simon ever had any true friends, that is.

"None of Dad's inventions ever made him any money, and that wasn't really the point for him. But there was one with the potential to be big. He invented a system for keeping cables under control. We were all busy buying electrical goods, and the number of cables hanging down behind tables or cupboards was multiplying. Dad's system was quite simple, but it worked. He talked to Simon about going for a patent and he offered to deal with it on Dad's behalf.

"Then they talked about starting a business to market the system. They didn't want to set up their own factory, but Simon had a contact in a place up north with the right equipment and spare capacity. Dad looked after the engineering side, developing the specifications and the drawings, doing the quality checks, while Simon looked after the sales and marketing side of things. Oh yes, and he provided most of the seed funding. Dad never had any spare money. He spent it all on us, or on his next prototype.

"For a few years, everything went well. No-one made a fortune, but Simon got all his investment back. Dad assumed they were now equal partners."

"And that wasn't the case?"

"Apparently not. They got an enquiry from an Indian company who wanted to buy the product and develop it into large scale manufacture. Dad was reluctant, but Simon persuaded him to sign an agreement. Poor Dad – he never saw them coming. Simon set up the deal so he got the lion's share of the profits and stole the rights to Dad's ideas. Simon Mountjoy was set up for life. He even featured in the Queen's New Year's honours list for services to industry!"

"And your father didn't try to get any restitution?"

"Not in his nature. And how could he fight against someone like that? Six months later, while he and Mum were on holiday in the Brecon Beacons, my father disappeared early one morning. He was always an early riser and often went for a walk on his own, so Mum wasn't worried to start with. But he never came back. His body was found three days later at the bottom of a waterfall, and it was assumed there'd been a tragic accident. And that's what the coroner recorded at the end of the inquest."

"But you don't believe it was an accident?"

"At first, I did. For years in fact. But then I saw Simon in the gym that day. He was on the treadmill, chatting to the bloke next to him. I didn't recognise him to start with. He'd put on weight and was looking even more prosperous than when we'd last seen him. He certainly didn't recognise me. But why would he? I was a child when he saw me before. Besides, in the gym, I was a member of staff, part of the furniture as far as he was concerned. I was able to get quite close to him without him realising I was listening to every word he said. And such interesting words they were too. He was boasting about some deal he'd done, back in London, that made him pots of money and allowed him to buy Mountjoy Manor. And I realised he was talking about Dad's invention."

"So you decided to take revenge? Is that why you came to Coombesford?"

"Not to start with, no. I was just glad he hadn't recognised me. But at Christmas, I was going through some of Dad's old papers, helping Mum have a clear-out. I found his last notebook tucked into a side pocket of his document case. And I realised from the final entries he'd been very depressed over Simon's betrayal. I now believe he took his own life."

"So what happened next, Mr Hughes?"

"A friend lives in Coombesford. We were having coffee one day and she mentioned Olga was looking to take on a personal trainer. My friend suggested I apply, and I got the job. At first, I just used to go there a couple of times a week. But we got on really well, and Olga suggested I took a room in the manor."

"Wasn't that a strange thing for her to do?"

"Not really. She's in a foreign country. She doesn't mix with the locals very much. And her husband was an older man who was more interested in that damn house than his wife. She was crying out for some company."

"When did you decide to kill him? Right from the start?"

"No. I never intended to kill him! My original intention was to see if I could get any dirt on the man. Maybe blackmail him. Get something for my mum."

"So what changed?"

"That bloody documentary. Simon showed us clips from it during the party at The Falls on the Saturday night. And then on the Sunday, he was boasting again about the deal that made him all his money and got him his CBE. He let slip there was someone else involved in the original design. One of the film crew asked him what happened to the other engineer. Had he invented anything else?" Nathan paused, biting his lip, before continuing, fighting back tears. "Simon laughed! Said he doubted it. The man was a loser, a dreamer. He said he had no idea where he was now." Nathan dropped his head into his hands and began to sob.

CHAPTER 38

DCI Harolds glanced at her sergeant and then looked back at the sobbing man across the table from her.

"I think we'll take a short break," she said, switching off the recorder. "Would you like a drink, Mr Hughes?"

Ten minutes later when the interview recommenced, Nathan Hughes was composed once more and continued to answer questions in a quiet, expressionless voice.

"So tell us what happened on the night of Sunday 7th July," asked the DCI.

"I was sitting out on the terrace when Simon arrived home. It was just gone eleven. Olga had gone to bed in a temper, having missed a night out with friends due to Simon going AWOL. He'd come around the side of the house because he was wearing his walking boots and didn't want to go through the house in them. I offered to fetch him some trainers from the porch and he poured us both a drink from the bar."

"What sort of mood was he in?"

"A bit strange, really. He'd been very quiet after that Iris woman came to see him in the afternoon. And he was still a bit moody when he arrived back. But after he'd had a drink, he suggested we go for a stroll around the garden."

"Was that usual?"

"No, it had never happened before. When I first moved in, he didn't really approve, although he never said no to anything Olga asked for. Then recently, he'd been a bit worried about his weight. Started talking about doing an exercise programme with me. I'd not really encouraged that. I didn't want to spend much time alone with him, but he was getting quite insistent."

"And what did you talk about as you walked around the garden?"

"Firstly about what he wanted to achieve from the new regime. He admitted he was worried about looking fat on television and wanted to lose some weight before the film crew came back later in the month for the rest of the filming. Then he started talking about the documentary again.

"I asked him how he'd managed to afford to buy Mountjoy Manor and get it back into shape. And he started telling me all about this deal he'd done with an Indian company. How he'd made loads of money out of that.

"'It must have been a good invention?' I said. 'Not my idea really, to be honest,' he said. 'Pinched it off some engineering guy with no business brains.' By then, we were standing by the stream looking down at the weirs. And all I could think of was my dad, throwing himself over the cliff in Wales and ending up at the bottom of a waterfall. Something snapped in my head. He turned away from me, I picked up a rock and hit him. And once I started, I couldn't stop! Then I pushed his body into the water, threw the rock in after him, watched him tumble over the weir, and went to bed."

DCI Harolds found her earlier pity for the young man fading with the realisation he seemed to feel no remorse for what he'd done.

"When you were caught in the hospital earlier, you were attempting to smother Ms Pauline Wilson," said DS Smith. "Can you tell us why?"

"She'd worked it out. Or at least she thought she had.

148

She's the friend I mentioned earlier, the one that told me about Olga looking for a trainer. When I was in Exeter, I used to volunteer at a respite centre for dementia patients and Pauline used to bring her mother in occasionally. We got talking one day and I found we had a lot in common. Not least, although she didn't realise it, our hatred for Simon Mountjoy. Once I moved to Coombesford, I used to have tea with her and her mum every so often.

"Olga and I had supper in The Falls last Thursday evening and I heard Pauline saying she knew Iris was innocent and she was going to tell the police. After supper, I popped over to see her. We had coffee and she told me she'd seen Iris getting out of Hilda's car around eight in the evening and boarding a bus for Bristol with a large bag. She then started going on about how Olga didn't have an alibi and how it was always someone close to home who was the murderer in the crime dramas she loved to watch. 'Unless of course it was you, Nathan,' she said with a laugh. But there must have been something in my face to give me away. Because she went very pale and jumped up from her seat. 'Oh my God,' she said, 'it was you. You killed Simon Mountjoy!' I got up and moved towards her. I was only going to try to explain to her, persuade her not to give me away. But she must have thought I was going to hurt her. She backed away from me, tripped over the edge of the carpet and fell, hitting her head on the fireplace. There was so much blood. I felt for a pulse but couldn't find one. I was convinced she was dead! I panicked. I was about to run away when I remembered the coffee cups. I rinsed them, put them in the sink and left."

"And when did you realise she was still alive?"

"When you were talking to Charlie and Annie in the bar yesterday morning. Olga wanted to talk to them about holding Simon's wake there, and asked me to pop in on my way back from my daily run. I was hot and sweaty, so didn't want to go through the front door. I went in round the back and was in the passageway when I heard you mention

Pauline's name. After that, I just wanted to get away without being seen, so I ran across the beer garden and up the path by the stream. I just knew I had to get to Pauline before she spoke to you!"

EPILOGUE: MONDAY 15TH JULY

It was mid-afternoon on Monday. The Falls didn't open for another couple of hours, and Charlie and Annie had invited a few folks around to celebrate Iris no longer being a suspect in Simon Mountjoy's murder. Charlie thought she looked slightly better than when the police had brought her back the week before, but not completely relaxed.

"She's been through a lot. She's bound to take a while to get over it," said Annie when Charlie commented on Iris's appearance.

"I guess you're right," Charlie replied, but she wasn't convinced. She thought there was something else troubling the woman. And she had a suspicion she knew what it was. But, if she was right, was it any of her business?

A while later, she was sitting outside in the car park having a sneaky cigarette. She knew it was a dreadful habit and she'd promised Annie she would give them up, but every once in a while… She heard the door creak behind her and a shadow fell on her. With a sigh, Iris sat down next to her on the garden wall.

"You'll be moving on, I guess?" asked Charlie. "Now this is all over?"

"Yes, I think so. Simon's gone and Olga isn't interested in getting to know me. I can't say I blame her. Why would she want to be saddled with a stepdaughter once removed? Especially one that's older then her."

"So where will you go next?"

"I haven't decided yet. Maybe France or Switzerland. Or even the Far East. There's so much to learn over there."

"Not to America, then?"

Iris gave a sharp intake of breath.

"No, I don't think so. Why would you think that?"

"Oh, I don't know. I just thought as that's where your birth father is?"

Iris jumped up and paced backwards and forwards across the car park in front of Charlie.

"Why would I want to see him? He's never even seen me. I'm nothing to him." She took another deep breath and smiled at Charlie. "No, I definitely think I'll head eastwards." She turned to walk back towards the pub, then stopped and looked back at Charlie. "Actually, I lied. I have already seen him. And he makes Simon Mountjoy look like an angel!

"My biological father was Adrian Fitzgibbons, Ade to his friends. As I told you the other day, he and my mum were married very briefly and I was the result. Or, strictly speaking, he and my mum were an item at university, I was the result, and their short-lived marriage was a consequence of me.

"After I'd trained as a chef and done quite a bit of travelling in Europe, I headed for the States and spent a couple of years there. And that was when I met Ade for the one and only time.

"Fitzgibbons is a relatively uncommon name and over the years, I'd periodically searched for him online. One of my idle Google searches came up with an Adrian Fitzgibbons, who was standing for mayor in a small town in the Midwest. It had to be him. The location was right. He didn't seem to have ventured very far from his original home town. And although this man was in his mid-fifties and way heavier than the young guy my mum married, I could still detect the family resemblance in his features.

"I travelled out there and signed up for a catering agency specialising in political and other high-visibility functions. It wasn't difficult to convince them of my experience and expertise, and of course, they just loved my accent!

"The night of our single meeting was a large fund-raiser. I'd helped with preparation of the food and then swapped places with one of the waiters serving the top table. Charlie, the man was gross. More than twenty-five stone by the look of him, and sweating like a pig under the lights. He'd been drinking pretty heavily since the function started, but it didn't seem to have affected him in any way. As I stood before him with a tray of *hors d'oeuvres,* he glanced up from the person he'd been listening to, and caught my eye. Next thing I knew, he'd grabbed my elbow and hissed in my ear to come back and see him at the end of the evening; we would have our own private party. My own dad was hitting on me!

"I smiled sweetly at him and walked away before I did or said something we would both regret. I left town that same night and three days later I was back in the UK. And one thing I decided as I flew over the Atlantic was it was time to stop hiding in the shadows and start facing my demons. I needed to go back to Surrey to see my grandparents before it was too late. And maybe it was also time to pay a visit to my stepfather. After all, I could well have been his heir, couldn't I?"

"So that's when you got in touch with Hilda?"

"Yes. I didn't want to just arrive on the doorstep unannounced. When Simon last saw me, my hair was cropped and dyed black, and I wore thick glasses. I was pretty sure he wouldn't recognise me after all this time, and I was right."

"Hilda told us she suggested you come and work for us."

"And it's been great fun, Charlie. I've really enjoyed working with you guys. But after the party the other weekend, I realised I couldn't put it off any longer. I went to see Simon on the Sunday afternoon."

"But it didn't go well." It was a statement rather than a question.

"You might say that. He shouted at me for disappearing, and refused to accept Mum's death was his fault. And then he accused me of being a gold-digger." Iris stopped and pulled a face. "Well, I suppose there was an element of truth to that. But whatever. I had to get away; Hilda helped me. I didn't know about Simon's death until I saw a bit in the newspaper on the Tuesday morning. And by then the police were onto me."

"Why didn't you just come clean to the police about who you were straight away, Iris?"

"Because I didn't know who'd killed him; and I was worried about dropping Hilda in it. And it gave me a motive for killing him." She shrugged. "It seemed logical at the time, anyway."

Charlie stood and held out her hand.

"Well, I wish you all the best, Iris, or should I say, Lily. I reckon you need a bit of good luck, don't you? But don't forget to keep in touch." Then there was a squeal and Suzy, just back from school, came rushing out and threw herself into Iris's arms. "Looks like the fan club's here. Let's go and get another drink."

That night after the pub had closed and Annie was already asleep in bed, Charlie sat at her laptop. She pulled up a couple of websites she'd consulted earlier and reread the article about a mayoral race in the Midwest being thrown into disarray when the front runner, one Adrian Fitzgibbons, had dropped dead suddenly at the end of a fundraiser. Cause of death was thought to be a dodgy oyster in the *hors d'oeuvres*. But Iris had talked about her birth father in the present tense. Unless she was a much better actor than they all realised, she had no idea he was dead.

Charlie closed everything down and stared at the desktop. Selecting a folder labelled Iris, her hand hovered for a few seconds over the keyboard. Then with a smile, she gently pressed the delete key, closed down the laptop and headed off to bed.

ENJOYED THIS BOOK?

Reviews and recommendations are very important to an author and help contribute to a book's success. If you have enjoyed *Murder at Mountjoy Manor* please recommend it to a friend, or better still, buy them a copy for their birthday or Christmas. And please consider posting a review on your preferred review site.

ACKNOWLEDGMENTS

I am once again very grateful for all the support provided by my friends in the thriving community of writers and readers, both in Devon and beyond.

In particular, my thanks go to Margaret Barnes for being my writing partner for the fourth time; to my friends in Chudleigh Writers' Circle and Exeter Writers; and to Carol Amorosi, Sue Anger, Jenny Benjamin, Jan Hill, Clare Lillington, Heather Morgan, Richard Morgan and Lisa S Plasse, my ever-patient beta readers.

Berni Stevens (bernistevenscoverdesign.com) is responsible for the beautiful cover and Otis Lea-Weston produced the detailed map of Coombesford. Julia Gibbs (@ProofreadJulia on Twitter) made sure the final text is as error-free as possible. My thanks go to all of them.

I also owe a huge debt of gratitude to my sisters, Margaret Andow and Sheila Pearson, for their analytical reading skills and ongoing cheerleading.

Finally, my thanks go, as always, to my husband Michael McCormick, my fiercest critic and strongest supporter, who continually asks me why I'm not at my desk, writing.

ABOUT THE AUTHOR

I was born and brought up in Birmingham. As a teenager, essays and poetry won me an overseas trip via a newspaper competition. Despite this, I took scientific and business qualifications and spent more than thirty years as a manufacturing consultant, business owner and technical writer before returning to creative writing in 2006. I have written short stories and poetry for competitions—and have had a few wins, several honourable mentions and some short-listing. I am published in several anthologies.

Under the Chudleigh Phoenix Publications imprint, I have published, in addition to my novels, three collections of my own short stories and another two co-authored with a friend. I also write non-fiction, including the *Author Business Foundations* series on business skills for writers running their own small business. My debut novel, *Gorgito's Ice Rink*, was runner-up in the 2015 Self-Published Book of the Year awards. The first in the Suzanne Jones series, *Counterfeit!*, came third in the 2015 Literature Works First Page Writing Prize.

I am editor of the Chudleigh Phoenix Community Magazine, and a member of Chudleigh Writers' Circle and Exeter Writers.

For more information on my writing, visit my website (elizabethducie.co.uk); follow me on Goodreads, Facebook, or Twitter; or watch the trailers for my books on YouTube.

Want to read more about the village of Coombesford and its residents? Readers of my newsletter get a free short story every month. Email me to sign up: elizabeth@elizabethducie.co.uk.

OTHER BOOKS BY ELIZABETH DUCIE

Coombesford Books
Villainy at the Village Store
Calamity at Coombesford Church
Coombesford Calander volume I
Coombesford Calendar volume II

The Jones Sisters series:
Counterfeit!
Deception!
Corruption!

Other fiction:
Gorgito's Ice Rink
Parcels in the Rain and Other Writing

Co-written with Sharon Cook:
Life is Not a Trifling Affair
Life is Not a Bed of Roses

Non-fiction:
Sunshine and Sausages

The Author Business Foundations series:
Part 1: Business Start-Up (ebook only)
Part 2: Finance Matters (ebook only)
Part 3: Improving Effectiveness (ebook only)
Parts 1-3 (print only)
Parts 1-3 Workbook (print only)
Part 4: Independent Publishing

Made in United States
North Haven, CT
16 December 2023

46022874R00100